Pete Paced the Court in the Darkened Arena.

"Vic, the championship banners don't win for us anymore. We need players. I need talent, athletes, horses. I'm coaching as good as I know how, and that isn't good enough anymore. We've got to have the horses."

"Thoroughbreds," answered Western University's Athletic Director.

"But half the coaches in the country are *buying* these high school players!" Pete thumped a fist into his palm. "Money under the table, cars, girls, whatever. And we all know it."

"Yup."

"It's illegal, it's unethical, it's immoral, it's—"

"Pete, calm down." Vic waggled his hands. "Nobody said you had to cheat. Winning runs in cycles. It'll come around again."

"Bull!" Pete swatted Vic's hands. "I ain't no Maytag. You know that's bull. Don't patronize me. We can't sit here waiting for a cycle. We have to get control." Pete stopped and chewed his lip for a moment. "However, there's two reasons I'm incapable of cheating. One, if I break the rules I might get busted and thrown out of coaching for the rest of my life, and that means I won't be drawing X's and O's for a bunch of kids I love. The fact is that all the bull of alumni and agents and shoe contracts and reporters is worth it if I teach these kids how to play basketball and, just a little bit, how to become men." He paused. "I could lose all the rest."

Vic waited. Pete seemed caught up in thought. "What's the second reason, Pete?"

Pete stared at him. "I might *not* get caught."

BLUE CHIPS ™

—— A Novel by ——
Richard Woodley
Based on the Motion Picture Written by
Ron Shelton

POCKET BOOKS

New York London Toronto Sydney Tokyo Singapore

This book is a work of fiction. Names, characters, places and
incidents are either products of the author's imagination or are used
fictitiously. Any resemblance to actual events or locales or persons,
living or dead, is entirely coincidental.

An *Original* Publication of POCKET BOOKS

POCKET BOOKS, a division of Simon & Schuster Inc.
1230 Avenue of the Americas, New York, NY 10020

ISBN: 0-671-89082-4

First Pocket Books printing March 1994

10 9 8 7 6 5 4 3 2 1

POCKET and colophon are registered trademarks of
Simon & Schuster Inc.

Printed in the U.S.A.

1

THE CHANCELLOR OF WESTERN UNIVERSITY SAT IN HIS usual seat on the aisle high above the arena floor, beneath the yellow vaulted steel beams that spread over the basketball scene like rays of Ra, enjoying what he believed was some commonality with his students.

"What is so difficult about winning?" he asked the aide seated next to him. "I mean, the chances are fifty-fifty right off the bat, aren't they? Two teams." He shrugged. "I like the way I heard it put the other day by a youngster: 'Just put the ball in the hole.' Rather crudely elegant, don't you think, Julian?"

The time-out was over, the Western University Dolphins, in blue and gold, resumed their offense against the Texas Western Sand Dogs, in gray and green. But the last few seconds of the first half were as fruitless for the home-team Dolphins as all the earlier minutes, and a pass to the pivot went through several hands and off two heads before thudding out of bounds against the padded backboard support as the buzzer went off.

As the teams trotted off, cheerleaders cartwheeled out to center court to celebrate halftime. The mascot, flabbily encased in a puffy gray outfit and looking as much like a shark or slug as a dolphin, scampered along the sidelines, eyes darting around deep inside the mouth, fin-arms flapping in exhortation as if trying to fly into the crowd.

"Do you think winning can be taught, Julian?"

Julian was leaning forward, his hands weighing his chin. "We just don't have the horses, I think."

"Ha! Tell that to the trustees. We have a tradition to uphold. Nothing wrong with winning. Get the horses. Coach the boys to put the ball in the hole." The chancellor considered this challenge. "Get me a Coke and one for yourself. Fine cheerleaders. Athletics is good."

Pete Bell leaned his blond head against the wall and snarled into the green cinder blocks. He could hear his team in the nearby locker room commiserating through growls, groans, and sniffs as they wound down from the first half and awaited his entry to chastise them and explain their ineptitude and propose a solution. Crowd noises sifted down through the

2

corridors and beset his ears. As inspiring as the crowd was when you were winning, it was stifling when you were losing. Everybody meant well. Everybody wanted the same thing. Well, almost everybody. Well, almost the same thing. Winning was so simple. Pete had always, throughout his career, been a winner. He couldn't explain the complexities of losing on a big-time college campus grown dependent on him for publicity, for income, and for stature.

The tap on his shoulder came from Mel Holly, one of his three assistant coaches, who then tapped his watch and nodded toward the locker room and continued on through the door. Pete followed.

If sweat were blood, this would be a trauma center. Sweat drenched the players and the benches on which they sat and the floor on which the benches sat; sweat trickled down the walls and fogged the air and dripped off the shower heads. Sweat was a sheen that covered everything like lacquer; sweat moistened the grunts and sighs and breaths that struggled to emerge and died in this heavy air. Sometimes, on winning nights, the sweat was the blood of brave and happy victors, bathing them with a fine mist of their own production, soothing them with the reward of battle richly done. But too often lately, like now, the sweat was cruel and suffocating, the loss of the sap of youth, a wicked miasma that crept up a man's nose like sewage with its expended human chemicals.

Pete stopped short, felt his eyes slam shut and his whole body clench and rock above his spread feet.

"Listen up!" he roared.

The hot room froze, a dozen young faces locked where they stared, breath momentarily sealed in tall, strong glistening bodies forced to rest. An instant of ominous quiet.

"How bad can it get?" Pete said, his eyes popping open as if blown by sparks. "I ask myself, how bad can it get?" He began to pace in the slow, measured, heavy steps of a patrolling ogre, wagging his head back and forth as he eyed the drooling ceiling. "I ask myself, is this the worst team that has ever sat in this locker room? Is that possible?"

Suddenly his head snapped down and he scanned their sullen faces with his burning eyes. "Huh? Is it possible that right here right now is the worst team ever? Somebody answer me!"

There were a few mumbles: ". . . pretty bad . . . stink . . . stupid jerks . . . disaster . . ."

"Shut up!" He stomped back and forth in front of them, fists jerking spastically. "You jerks don't deserve a locker room this year." He went to the open door, ripped off the plastic Dolphins sign, flung it clattering down the hall, slammed the door, whirled again to face them. "You don't deserve uniforms!"

There was some unpleasant squirming; a few high-top Man-o'-War sneakers squeaked on the rubber floor mat. Eyes found lower levels.

Pete paused, continuing to pace slowly. It was important that he not run out of steam. He lowered his voice some.

"Every time we play a game I want to throw up. I'm

4

sick of watching you guys play. Not one of you in this room has learned how to win. Not one! The last four games we got hammered. Now this! Keep playing the way we're playing and we're gonna get our butts whipped again. I'm tired of it, of fighting you jerks. You're the dumbest team I ever coached. I am so depressed I don't even want to talk about it."

He spread his arms toward his three assistants. "You guys think of something!"

He stormed out of the locker room, slammed the door behind him, and leaned his forehead against the wall.

He used to have a magic touch with this, bringing them up short to get their awed attention, then charging into the nuts and bolts of the game, then razzing them into a confident fever to launch the second half. But it was different when they were winning. Because then you didn't try to fool them by telling them they stunk; you insisted that they could play better, that the game was still up for grabs, and then you could concentrate on the execution of the game itself—the mechanics and imagination and fundamentals at which he really excelled—the plays they should run on offense, the plays they should look out for on defense, zones, man-to-man, high and low posts, touch passes, back-door cuts, outlet passes, box-outs, communication, eyes-eyes-eyes. And then, finally, dig deep, guys, play through the exhaustion, never never let down, be proud when you walk off the court.

That kind of scheme. He loved playing the short

halftime rhythm, timing everything just right, returning them to the floor on just the right note. He relished
his ability to condense his knowledge into edible
bites, and how his players hungrily responded. But
now he felt a sudden brief panic because he had
nothing to work with, to build upon. The problem was
not that they were so bad—mercy, they could still
beat most teams in this big United States—but that
they needed to be so good. The national championship was always supposed to be within their grasp;
something close to the top was absolutely expected by
the administration, the students, and the alumni. A
season with more losses than wins was almost unim-
aginable on this hallowed campus that had for so long
set the standard for the country and asserted the
preeminence of college basketball finally on the West
Coast.

Yet here they were on the very lip of the abyss, a
group of tall and talented athletes who had come here
a year or two or three ago expecting to win, who by
and large went to classes just in case they didn't make
it into the NBA, a politically acceptable mix of white
and black players who got along well and worked hard.
Here they were, about to fail.

They just weren't good enough. Pete hated to admit
to himself that it was getting harder to do what he did
best: persuade brilliant high school players to come to
Western for no other reason than to play for him and
get a fine education, and then teach them how to play
the very best team basketball so they could win even
against the toughest schedule anywhere. These were

great kids, just like always. They just weren't great basketball players.

Unless he himself was slipping.

Naw.

Inside the locker room, the three assistants—Mel Holly, a chubby black man and the one who had known Pete the longest; Freddie Pinyon, a somber string bean from Maryland; and Jack Garf, an intense, bald strategist who'd been around the Big Ten for years before coming here—huddled casually in the corner.

"We gonna play more zone?" Freddie asked nervously.

"We got to run and trap," Jack said, spitting between his teeth into the drainage gutter at the base of the wall.

"He'll be back," Mel said, "so let's just cool it."

"I never seen him quite this way, though," Freddie said.

"We never been quite so bad."

"Probably couldn't trap these guys either," Jack muttered. "What we ain't got in height we also lack in speed."

Suddenly Pete banged back through the door and strode to the center of the room and looked around from player to player. "Honestly, I just want to go home and cry when I see us play. Don't you guys understand? I want this so bad I can taste it! Don't you guys want what I want? Don't you guys want to be good? Basketball is the toughest game in the world to play. You have to be able to think on every possession.

You beat people through execution; you don't beat them just because you outjump them, outrun them or outshoot them. You outthink them! You outexecute them! Tony!"

Tony Macklin, the quiet six-foot-four-inch junior point guard charged with running the team on the floor, looked up warily, wishing he could be back in Chicago just for the next couple of minutes. "Yeah, Coach?"

"Are we executing?"

"Not really."

"Are we a team that stands around with our thumbs in our mouths?"

"Not supposed to be."

"We hurry the ball up-court, do we not?"

"Yes we do."

"We don't wait for the other team to get set, do we?"

"Nope."

"We don't stand around."

"Nope."

"And you, Tony, are protecting the ball like it's gold, like it's the payroll, Tony, you're guarding and delivering the payroll! You have the money, Tony. Do you understand?"

"The money, yes sir."

"So what accounts for us being down ten at the half to a Texas team you never heard of before you came here?"

"Uh . . ."

"Mike?"

Michael Nover, the broad-shouldered six-foot-six-inch power forward, ran his hand over his crew cut. "We stink."

"Chuck?"

Chuck was the bad-kneed six-foot-eight-inch center who had started out with such promise and seemed to get worse during each of his three years. "Execute!"

Pete spun away and gritted his teeth. "Push the ball up, Tony, distribute it, move, move the club! Is this so difficult? I have never had a losing season, and I will not have one. The only joy for me is I only have to watch you guys play one more game!"

His eyes swam. Nothing was happening.

"I can't tell you how sick I am of basketball right now," Pete growled on. "I never thought I'd see the day when Western basketball was in the state it's in right now. If I never see another game in my life, that will be just fine."

"Yes . . . yes . . . got that right."

Swearing, he charged over to the corner and grabbed the video projector and threw it against the wall and felt miserable listening to the silence that followed the crash and scattering of tiny components. He ran across the room and kicked the rack of basketballs, sending them hopping in all directions. He was helpless. "You can coast through college. You can coast through life. But I guarantee you, you can't win without trying. I want to win this game! Let's go!"

The players jumped to their feet and dodged through the ricocheting balls and sprinted up the corridor toward the court.

Mel sidled up to walk beside Pete. "What do you think?"

"Nothing."

"Got to trap," Jack said.

"Yeah, yeah." Pete ground his teeth and found a cavity that zinged him like a message from God.

When they reentered the arena, the crowd was boisterous. Up in the stands behind the bench fifty members of Pete's Posse, as they called themselves, wearing dolphin heads, swung rhythmically to the rock music of the pep band and the sexy sashaying of the cheerleaders.

"They still believe," Pete muttered.

The mascot came prancing over and stopped. Pete thought that if he didn't get out of his face with those flickering eyes down in the throat that he just might pop him in the shiny, flat beak.

He looked away, glancing around the stands, flashing past the chancellor and other muck-a-mucks, until he spotted a man in sunglasses and a trench coat standing half hidden in an aisle.

He closed his eyes. "Slick Phil," he grumbled to himself, "thinks he's some kind of spy."

The team gathered around him, smacked hands together in the middle, agreed they were gonna go get 'em, and went out to begin the second half.

Pete sat down next to Mel in the folding chair closest to the scorer's table, while the substitutes wandered to their chairs down the row.

More of the same. Even though Pete had allowed himself to believe there was a chance, as he always allowed himself to do, on this night when nothing was happening. There was no magic.

Tony ran a lazy cut off the high post, and the defender was all over him and stole the pass and triggered an immediate Texas fast break. At the opposite end their guard pulled up and drilled a twelve-footer.

"Transition!" Pete bellowed. "Mel, didn't we talk about transition?"

"We talked about everything."

Tony, embarrassed by having had a previous pass stolen, tried to beat a backcourt double-team all by himself, dribbling through his legs.

"Help out, help out!" Pete sprang up and waved frantically to bring players back.

Tony spun and twisted, looking for an outlet, while the two defenders slapped at his arms.

"They're killing him!" Pete hollered at the ref. "Come on, Earl, call something! You need to see blood?"

"Sit down," the ref said, motioning Pete toward the chair as he called a jump ball.

The game continued its inexorable path toward the team's fifth straight loss.

The Texas guard dribbled into the corner.

"Trap, trap, trap!" shouted the four coaches in unison.

But the Western defenders were slow. The guard slipped free and passed underneath for a layup.

"We've gone over and over that trap a thousand times," Pete said, "and these clowns still don't get it."

"Monkey see, monkey don't do," Mel said.

The game wore on, and the Dolphins were unable to chip into the Texas Western lead. The crowd became quieter, allowing more raucous individual voices to penetrate: "C'mon, move the ball! . . . Open your eyes! . . . Get some shooters out there!"

The point guard, Tony, was showing frustration, becoming more fiery, driving more aggressively. He brought the ball up-court and elbowed aside the defender who was crowding him.

"Charging!" the referee sang. "Four-four white." He flashed four fingers twice, indicating Tony's number. Tony slapped the ball in disgust.

Pete jumped up to make a *T* with his hands, signaling a time-out, and advanced a couple of steps onto the court. "Hey, ref, call 'em both ways! The guy had no position!"

The referee sidled over. "Back off or I'm gonna ring you up."

Pete swore as he turned away to join the sideline huddle during the time-out.

"Tony," he said to his point guard, "you gotta take charge out there, but you can't do it all. Don't let them get to you. You make a mistake, put it behind you. You're overplaying, overanxious. Be cool. . . . Matt."

A white boy in the huddle looked up.

"Just because you're white doesn't mean you can't *try* to jump. I mean, you're supposed to hit the boards. You *used* to hit the boards, our best bounder. Don't let these redneck slobs intimidate you."

"The refs aren't letting us—"

"*I'll* worry about the refs. You just play basketball. . . . Michael."

He addressed a broad-shouldered, power forward from the Dominican Republic.

"What'sa matter? You lose your nerve? Ball's loose on the floor, you don't just bend from the waist like a ballet dancer—you drop and go for it! Oh man, oh man." He shook his head and looked at another player.

"Chuck, it's called a basketball. It's the round thing out there. It bounces." Chuck remained stone-faced as Pete raced on. "Look, boys, they just went to the corner and we didn't trap. When the ball's in the corner we've got 'em. Nobody's in the passing lane, we're standing around, and our hands aren't up. Now let's get out there and execute."

As the teams stacked hands before rejoining the fray, Happy Kuykendall joined the chancellor in the stands. Wearing a blue blazer over a white shirt with a blue tie with gold dolphins on it, Happy, a wealthy man retired from his own insurance business, was one of the more active alumni.

"I don't like the way things are going, chief," he said.

"Well, they're trying." Chancellor Millar nodded hopefully. "To put the ball in the hole."

"You know how proud we all our of our alma mater."

"Sure do, Happy, surely."

"Losing hurts us, right here." He thumped a fist against his chest. "We've been losing a lot. What do you think about the coach? Any thoughts?"

"Well . . ."

"I mean, it's either the coaching or the players, isn't it? And the coach gets the players. So . . ."

"Rocky stretch, all right. Maybe we'll win this one."

"Pete's hot." Happy gestured toward the floor.

The ref had called a blocking foul on Tony, and Pete was stomping up and down in front of his bench, hands on hips, leaning out to bellow at the culprit. "What's that, Earl! You blind? Ray Charles could've made that call! You keep your eyes in your pants!"

"Technical foul on Bell," the ref announced toward the scorer's table, making a *T* with his hands. "That's one, Pete. Take it easy."

"What!" Pete threw up his hands. "What? 'Cause of Ray Charles? 'Cause of a joke? You keep your brains with your eyes!"

"Technical on Bell, number two, automatic ejection!" Earl made the *T*, then pointed grandly in the general direction of the locker room.

Pete grabbed the ball out of Earl's hands, jogged a couple of steps, and punted it high up into the stands, where it whanged around the seats as people ducked.

Earl flapped his index fingers wildly, as if they were a pair of six-shooters. "Get into the locker room, Pete, you maniac! 'Fore you kill somebody!"

Pete turned calmly to his assistants. "Go to half-court traps and jam the lanes. Fall back into a pressure man-to-man. Overplay like crazy even if we get

14

burned a couple times. And keep the ball in Tony's hands. Have him start putting it up himself.

"Pete!" Earl barked into his ear.

"I'm going, I'm going." As he walked briskly toward the locker room, Pete waved to the crowd and received a roaring cheer back, mixed with boos for the refs.

"They still believe." Pete chuckled bitterly.

2

HEY." VIC ROKER, THE ATHLETIC DIRECTOR AND ONE-time basketball coach, stepped into the steam room wearing a towel around his waist. Vic, at fifty-six, was half a dozen years older than Pete, and a good fifty pounds heavier, with pecs that had sagged to breasts, belying his college days as a football fullback.

"Hey," Pete said without looking up. He leaned forward, forearms on the towel across his knees, and would have been staring at the floor except that his eyes were closed.

"Are you a maniac?"

"I got a toothache."

Vic sat next to him on the wooden bench and assumed a similar position. "As the A.D. of this

16

distinguished institution, I feel obliged to comment officially on your behavior on the basketball court this evening."

"Go ahead, Vic."

"You still got a good leg, Pete. That ball musta gone forty rows up." Vic chuckled. "Not quite as good as three years ago, though, at that Louisville game. That baby must've gone sixty-five rows, all the way to the cheap seats."

"I used to kick better."

"Yeah. Yeah." Vic watched Pete rise and move to the door. "What's up?"

"Toothache."

"I mean what else?" Vic followed him out, toweling off.

Pete shrugged.

They stepped into the showers briefly, then dressed and retired to the coaches' office.

"Actually, I thought the kids played pretty well tonight," Vic said, settling into the sofa across the room from Pete, "as well as they could."

"Maybe."

"Maybe! Look, Pete, nobody could get as much outta these kids as you. Nobody."

"Yeah? Well, if that's true, if I have to work this hard to get the kids to play at this level—this lousy—I don't know if I can go through another game."

"Keep in mind the competition, Pete, the schedule we play. They aren't so lousy."

"Oh, yeah? Brass and boosters expect us to win. I

expect us to win. That's why I'm here. Otherwise I'd be coaching at some calm and gentle backwater where nobody gave a rap. I'd get up in the morning with a song on my lips, have fun practices, win a game once in a while, and just do as I pleased. We play a top schedule. We used to win at the top."

"Hey, it's the end of a long season." Vic spread his arms like an evangelist. "You'll feel better in the morning."

"I'll feel worse. Reality at dawn. Tell you what." Pete ran his tongue around his back teeth, tickling for the source of pain. "If I don't shape up this program, Vic, we keep playing like this, you're gonna lose your cushy job."

"I've thought about that." Vic smiled wanly.

"They always fire the old guys first. Thought about that? A.D.s are an easy mark, great scapegoats."

"Old? Look at you. You've aged twenty years this season."

"Oh?" Pete went to the medicine cabinet, took two pills from a small bottle, and swallowed them down. "That what you're telling people? One more game like this and I'll be older than you."

"Please. That aspirin?"

"Who wants to know?"

"Because if it is, I wish you'd drink some water with it so you don't bleed to death internally."

"Know what the trouble with you is, Vic? You worry about the wrong things. Game's over." Pete grabbed his jacket and started for the door.

"How do you know?"

"Listen." Pete cupped a hand to his ear. "What you hear is the silence of another burial."

"Heads up, guys!" Pete barked as he strode through the locker room where the defeated players sagged in various poses of dejection and sighed and cursed and wheezed under their breath. "You lose, you do not slink off the floor with your tail between your legs!"

He slapped players on the back and tapped their heads and chucked them under their drooping chins. "Come on, come on! We ain't babies here. Get it together! It's just one game. We got jobbed by the refs, worst officiating I've seen in fifteen years. But this game is history. We start preparing for C.U. right now."

A final collective sigh seemed to rouse the boys, and several looked up while they continued to tug off their soppy uniforms.

"They got a great low-post game and two quick guards who can penetrate and shoot off the dribble. They're a better team than they were when we lost in overtime earlier this year. Right now we gotta start thinking about slowing down their transition game."

He turned to his assistants. "Run 'em through it, Mel. I gotta go diddle the press."

Pete felt like a fraud as he headed toward the interview room. Or at least he felt unsure. It was a confusion he had never felt before, and he was trying to identify it. It was getting harder and harder to recruit the best of the corps of high school players against growing competition from more and more colleges that were offering more and more of who knew what. He had always felt that there were enough players across the board who were close enough to the best so that he could meld them together and produce winners. That was what he had always done. And once you were national champions, the job got easier. But everything happened faster now: TV was giving wider exposure; money followed the TV; players no longer stayed home or even in their home areas; school administrations were in a hurry; nobody had any patience to develop winners anymore. You had to win now. Right away and all the time. No respite. Fortunes depended on it. *Education* depended on it—the basketball program erected buildings and provided equipment, just like the football program. You couldn't have a great science program without a great athletic program. Or so it seemed. And schools were ever more willing to invest great sums in the pursuit of sports.

He strode into the cramped room and stepped up on the platform and stood before the blue and gold dolphin logo and stared past the microphones at the wriggling eels of the press. Forty or fifty of them, big lights and cameras at the rear, broadcasters standing with mikes, writers seated on folding chairs. Men in sport jackets, women—there were maybe a dozen, all of them great-looking, some of them with brains, higher percentage of women with brains than men—

in blazers and skirts. He didn't know why he despised the press so. Well, he didn't despise them individually, just as a group. He knew they were just doing their job, as they often reminded him. But they were doing it without knowing what you had to know to get it right. They didn't know the many subtle problems with which he had to deal and the players had to deal. They didn't know about special coach-player relationships, girlfriends, minor injuries, personal problems, parents.

"All right," he said, bringing them to attention. "First, my congratulations to Texas Western and its coaching staff. They played hard, stuck to their game plan, executed. But you saw the game, so you write about it, whatever you want. Any questions, stupid or otherwise?"

Generally he got along fine with them. They liked his gruffness. And he had long ago assumed the status of an icon because he had produced national champions. He was *famous*. And while he might not answer every question, he didn't lie.

A young newspaperman whose name Pete couldn't remember stood up warily. "Coach, you got ejected for technicals at a crucial time in the game. Could you explain why? Was it intentional, like maybe to jar the team and get them going, or—"

"In a game there's no time that's not crucial. You add it *all* up at the end, all the buckets, all the mistakes. I thought the refs were blowing some calls. You know I don't do *anything* intentionally. Next?"

After a scattering of chuckles, a woman with long auburn curls raised her hand. "Coach, would you like to give us your side of the ball-kicking incident?"

"My side? What other side is there? I took the ball and booted it as far and as high as I could because I thought it would be safer up there than in the hands of either the refs or the Dolphins. I was reasonably satisified. I'm told I had good leg extension, but I don't have the follow-through I used to have. In my prime I could reach the rafters easy."

Everyone laughed. Except for one, a willowy, stoop-shouldered, curly-haired, scowling writer nearly Pete's age who rose with the casual weariness of a battle-worn attorney.

"Speaking of your prime, Coach Bell, it's no secret that you've had recruiting problems in recent years. Is it fair to say that these problems began two years ago after the alleged point-shaving incident?"

You slime! That was what Pete wanted to say to Ed Axelby, who missed no opportunity to hurl nasty innuendos just in the hope of getting a good out-of-control quote. Pete always tried to parry these cynical stabs with offhand wit, but sometimes Axelby got to him.

"There was no point-shaving incident two years ago, or any other time, and you know it. And everybody who knows the program knows it!"

"Well . . ."

"There was only an 'alleged' incident because you invented it—like if I assert that you sleep with sheep, then it is 'alleged' that you sleep with sheep!"

"That's out of line, sir!"

"If you can't stand the heat, get out of my face!" The veins in Pete's neck stood out as he leaned forward over the mikes, almost on tiptoes, his jaw jutting out farther still. He ground his teeth, and a bolt of pain shot up his jaw to his ear. He winced and leaned back and took a deep breath.

"Look," he said. "We can't force 'em to come here, and we don't pay 'em to come here. We still attract good players. We lost tonight because we had some players who played poorly. Or because I failed as a coach. Or because the point spread was all wrong to start with. But I don't deal with point spreads, I deal with young men who go to school and graduate and do the best they can on the basketball court. Winning breeds winning, losing breeds losing. We won clean, we're losing clean. Anybody here can look me in the eye and know that nothing like point-shaving could happen here as long as I'm happening here."

"I'm not saying it happened," Ed Axelby said grumpily. "I'm only asking you if the allegations have hurt recruiting."

"No."

A couple of hands went up.

"If you people can't come up with better questions than this, the press conference is over. You guys all saw the game. Go write your stories. I got work to do."

Outside the locker room door he almost stumbled over the crumpled figure of the Dolphin mascot squatting against the wall with his head down. Dark splotches gathered on his gray dolphin chest, drops falling off his beak.

"Oh, brother," Pete muttered. "Come on, big guy, suck it up and hold the tears. The mascot can't get down."

"Sorry, Coach."

Pete tapped the gray head with his knuckles like rapping on a drum, and saw Mel turn the corner headed toward him, carrying a pair of videocassettes.

"Game tapes, Pete. Pretty ugly."

Pete took the black cassettes and frowned at them as if they had spoken. "Well, I won't be surprised, since I saw the game."

"Want some company? A beer?"

"Naw. I'd be rotten company."

"You're never rotten company. Pain in the neck, maybe. Not rotten."

"Think I'll take a walk. Thanks, though."

Mel flicked his finger in a good-bye, and Pete went out into the cool, clear night.

It was quiet. He liked the contrast from the arena. He loved crowds when his players were winning, solitude when they lost. More and more he liked solitude. He didn't want to explain anything. It was tough enough to figure it out. There was something reassuringly solid about concrete after all that thumping on the hardwood floor. Quiet.

"Watch where you're going!" The fender actually brushed his pants as the car rounded the corner and sped on. He sprang back onto the curb and stood sputtering as the car disappeared before he could think of any good names to call it. "Whew. Eyes, Pete, eyes."

He walked on, a bit more alert now, his videotapes in his hand. He had walked quite a while, he realized, quite a ways. Across the street was a playground, lit up, with a full-court game in progress. He stopped and watched for a few seconds, quickly picking up ages, sizes, talent level, wondering what kind of jobs people had that allowed them to play basketball at this wee hour. "Man, I'm tired of basketball." He spat and turned away.

He was passing a vacant lot when he spotted on the broken sidewalk yellow markings for hopscotch, and off to the side a stub of yellow chalk. Impulsively he squatted, put down the cassettes, took the chalk, and began scratching *X*'s and *O*'s on the concrete, diagramming plays: cuts off a high post, off a low post; back-door cuts. Disgusted with himself, he slammed the chalk to the ground and stalked off into the night.

The neighborhood was familiar and comfortable. Unsettling at the same time, full of memories. He walked across the friendly grass and up to the door of a trim and substantial brick ranch house that backed up to the edge of a canyon, and rang the bell. He rang it just once, then waited a long time. He knew she would come.

"Hi, Jenny. You see the game?" he asked, striding in as casually as he could, purposefully taking the room.

"No rebounding. You got beat on the boards."

"Among other things." She was lovely, with her brown hair tousled from sleep, hugging her old red terry-cloth robe around her as if it were a straitjacket. Her eyes were smudged, which made them especially erotic. He looked at her and was suddenly tongue-tied, glad she spoke.

"Actually, I thought your kids played their hearts out."

"Yeah. We're small and slow, an unbeatable combination. But they try, they try."

"Maybe you should've pressured their guards more, done some trapping. But what do I know? What're you doing?"

Pete slid a tape into the VCR and leaned over to study the buttons, not answering.

"Hey, come on, no game tapes now. Not tonight, Pete."

Pete popped the tape back out. "Sorry. . . . I . . ." he shook his head and reached underneath into the cabinet and snatched up a bottle of Glenlivet and a glass. He quickly poured a generous shot and tossed it down.

"That's the good stuff, Coach," she said with a wry smile. "If you're going to drink like a fish, I have some cheap stuff above the refrigerator."

He didn't look at her. "I wasn't planning on having a lot. I got a toothache."

"Still . . ."

"You trying to slow me down?" He glanced at her over his shoulder, trying not to feel defensive.

"Always."

"You're right. No need to rush it." He enjoyed the double meaning, hoping she didn't notice. He poured another drink and sat down in the recliner, swirling the drink gently. She hadn't moved. "So, how was your day?"

"My day?" She eyed him quizzically. "I taught thirty-five first graders how to cut out valentines. It was excruciating."

"Yeah. Hearts are tough to cut out."

"They're easier than pumpkins." She moved toward him. "What's the matter?"

"I wish you'd sit down, at least. I feel like you're standing there with a rolling pin, tapping your foot."

She sat on the sofa and curled her bare feet up under her. "Okay. Tell me."

"It's that Axelby. He's on me like a chigger, going after the 'alleged incident' again. I'd like to swat him."

"You can't let him get to you. Nothing new, right? Just a rehash of the old lies. Let go of it?"

"Jenny, I'm looking at my first losing season. It's getting to me. Then that skinny bugger comes along scattering his buckshot—"

"Pete . . ." She got up and paced around, head down, pushing away with her hands as if groping through a crowd.

"Yeah, yeah. It's late."

"Not just that. You picked up a double technical

that gave Texas Western a seven-point run. What about that? If one of your kids lost control like that, you'd sit his butt right down."

"I know. I know."

"Well, don't you think it's a bit much for a fifty-year-old man to be kicking balls into the stands?"

"Hey, I had to kick something. Balls are good." He chuckled, then spread his arms. "That ref made me mad. He's not fit to call a game in a summer camp for eight-year-olds." He swirled his drink and looked down into it. "How far did it go? I hope it didn't hit anybody."

"No, it didn't hit anybody, but it went farther than the one you kicked against Louisville three years ago."

"Don't you get it, Jenny? The program's in deep trouble!"

"Oh, please." She turned away for a moment, then back. "Pete, you've won two national championships —that's two more than most coaches dream of. You've won eight conference titles. Is that losing? You got great kids in the cleanest program in America, kids that graduate. You make a lot of money doing exactly what you want to do. I could go on."

"Go on, go on."

"No. Because I'll get angry and you like it when I get angry."

"Yeah, I do. It makes you beautiful."

She crossed her arms.

He took a step toward her and softened his voice. "Tell me again, why are we divorced?"

She smiled, warmly now. "Because you are impossible to live with."

He nodded briskly. "But besides that . . ."

"The door, Coach. I'm showing you the door."

"Yeah. Not for the first time."

"And, Pete, probably not for the last either. 'Night."

3

You know I love you, Evonda," Tony said. "How can you think different?"

Evonda pouted on the sofa in her aunt's house not far from campus. "Now you got what you wanted."

"No, Evonda, it's not like that. I'm not like that at all. I'm here, right?"

"You rather be playin' ball. Always playin' ball. When you win, be with the guys, when you lose, come over here and be crabby. Nothin' but ball for you in your life."

"Aw, Evonda." He tried again to put his arm around her shoulders; again she pushed him away. "It's my *job*. I mean, it's gonna be my job, if I'm good enough. I'm just a kid, Evonda. We're just kids. I got to get where I'm going to get now, while I got a chance.

And that's playin' ball, that's all. Better'n driving a bus or hauling coal."

"Don't nobody haul coal, junior, not no more."

"My granddaddy hauled coal."

"Well, today's today. And you've changed. You used to be more fun."

"I used to *have* more fun, baby. Basketball used to be more fun. It's work, that's what it is."

"And then you go and lose."

"I do the best I can."

"So you say. You're different, though. You ain't happy with it. So what's the point?"

"Money, doll. Someday. Next year, maybe. Scouts come to the games. I could play in the NBA."

"So you say. All's I know is that I talk about real life and what's goin' on, and what's goin' on with *me*, and all you see is you either had a good game or you had a bad game, and you 'spect me to pick up the slack. I ain't gonna grow old this way, mister."

"Evonda, you're only eighteen. How can you talk like that?"

"'Cause you get old quick in this game, bein' a girl."

"Me too, Evonda." This time he clamped her shoulders quickly before she could shove him off. "Old comes fast in basketball. Got to make it while you make it."

"Well, Tony, here we are growin' old together, and I ain't even been young yet."

"Evonda!" came her aunt's voice from upstairs. "You get yourself up here to bed. Now, girl!"

* * *

31

"D'you see that Latvian drive the baseline, Mel? You see that? Wow, can he go or what? Muscles on his muscles."

Mel Holly turned his draft beer mug slowly in his hands as he gazed up at the TV screen hanging over the end of the bar. "I think they can beat the Knicks this year, with that guy. This is the Lakers' year."

Jack Garf nodded, pursing his lips, enjoying the company of a good basketball man—and incidentally the assistant coach closest to Coach Bell, a conduit Jack liked to cultivate because he thought one day he might himself get that job. "And can he pop from outside or what? I mean, he can pop from thirty, forty feet, right? Sterno, or however you pronounce his first name. How did they learn how to play basketball in Latvia, Mel?"

Mel shrugged and flattened his hand over his mug as the bartender came by, silently asking. "Same way as here, I guess. How else?"

"Yeah, but I mean, how did they get a game together in a place like that, way over there where there's no natural basketball? What do you suppose they eat over there? Where is Latvia, anyway? Over by Russia someplace, right? That's probably where they picked it up."

"Everybody's got TV now, Jack. The whole world. We sure could use some of that talent in our house, if they got more like him."

"Yeah." Jack emptied his mug and signaled for another. "Hey, Mel, where do you think we are, exactly, right now, with our program?"

"Doldrums."

"Is Pete losing it, if you don't mind me putting it that way? Just between you and me, right? You know how much I love the guy."

There was a "Whoop!" and a bunch of shrieks and cheers over at the pool table.

"Man, the world is getting youthful," Mel said, glancing around, a chuckle shaking his big belly.

"I mean, you think he's getting out of touch?"

"He won't bend, that's all."

"You mean run and trap more?"

"Naw. He's still the best coach in the country. He'd run and trap more if he had the players to run and trap with. Naw. He won't bend the program to get the players."

"You mean he won't go get 'em, like some places, if you know what I mean."

"I know what you mean."

"I mean, he *tries* to get 'em, but he won't, you know . . ." Jack demonstrated with his hands as if dealing cards. "If you get my drift."

"I get your drift."

"I mean, with some of those, uh, inner-city kids, you know, know what I mean? I mean the have-nots, those really big, fast kids—all the young Michael Jordans—they don't have anything, you know? Some don't even have food, you know? You have to be able to . . ." Again he dealt with his hands.

"Jack, not all black kids are young Michaels. Not necessarily. A lot of them are broke, that's true. It's also true that they have generally liked playing for Pete Bell."

"Now, Mel, no offense, right? You know—"

"None taken, Jack." Mel chortled. "We know each other too well for that. And maybe you got a point, too, about kids running a tougher bargain than they used to—or their agents or papas or whatever—what with so many schools upping the ante all over the place. But tell you what, I'm not sure Pete should change. I'm not sure he should bend. I'm just not clear about that."

"It's a philosophical question, right, Mel?"

"Basketball question. What kind of team we want to put out there? What kind of attitude? What kind of kids? But it's a fair question, all right. I just don't have the answer. Guess I'll go however Pete goes on it. I gotta get home."

Mel slid his ample butt off the barstool and clapped Jack on the back. "Just keep in mind, old buddy, that Pete knows all about it. It ain't a secret question. Maybe he doesn't have the answer either."

"But winning is uppermost, right? I mean, that's what the game is all about."

"Yup. Games are about winning. And that happens just exactly fifty percent of the time, same as losing, philosophically speaking."

"Come again?"

"See you tomorrow."

Pete shivered involuntarily at the lonely sound of the night surf as he approached the small cottage that had become his home. He tried to think thoughts of pleasure and promise, but none would come to him now, and he was stuck with just being Pete Bell, age fifty, coming home to an empty house after another loss.

He opened the door and flipped on the light and was greeted by the same scenery that had welcomed him for all his recent days: a depressing clutter of magazines and newspapers and clothes strewn around on the faded orange fabric of his rented furniture. Sneakers in various stages of disrepair were scattered around the floor, along with socks and underwear.

"What a palace," he mumbled as he walked quickly through the room. A bachelor pad, all right. A solid reminder. The worst part of it was that it was not like him at all, not like what he remembered about how it used to be. He had always been basically neat, well ordered, and organized. Until he came here and just let things slide. So the cottage was all the more firm a reminder of how his life had changed.

He went into the kitchen and opened the refrigerator. It stank. In it were several cans of Coors beer, a few disheveled packages of anonymous cheese, half a bag of pretzels, two containers of Colombo yogurt. The stink wasn't from him; the refrigerator had stunk when he moved into the place. He'd thought he would get used to it, but it was like a slap in the face every time he opened the door.

He grabbed a beer and headed for the bedroom. He piled up three pillows at the head of the unmade bed and flopped down, his fingers quickly finding the remote control next to him. He clicked on the TV to the all-night sports channel.

". . . and in closing," the reporter was saying, "it's time to call 'em like we see 'em, and Coach Petey Bell of the Western University Dolphins has clearly lost the touch he once had . . ."

"Prissy, self-righteous, pretty-boy," Pete muttered.

". . . This year's team may be the least disciplined, least fundamentally sound squad we've seen in years. And Bell's preposterous sideline antics are boorish. They are becoming an embarrassment. Message to Athletic Director Vic Roker: It's time to dump Pete Bell, and bring somebody in here who's more in step with the times."

"In step with the times!" Pete sprang up from the bed, grabbed a cassette, and jammed it into the VCR. "You arrogant punk! What do you know about the times, let alone basketball? I'll show you fundamentals, you ignorant simp!"

Still muttering, he sagged back down on the bed, aimed the remote, and started the game film rolling in the VCR.

"No, no, no, Tony!" Pete called, halting the scrimmage. "That cross-court pass has to be quick. Don't telegraph it. Again!"

They started moving the ball around, players cutting this way and that. There was bumping and stumbling.

"Michael, what are you doing?" Pete strode into the

middle of the mess and snatched the ball out of the quiet forward's hands. "Eyes, Mike, eyes! Don't turn your head away. Compton is quick, your man'll be gone. Again!"

They swung into action. A shot went up from the side, bounced off the rim, then was rammed home on a slam dunk.

"Chuck! What're you doing? How can you not box out on that shot? You're facing the shooter. You watch him taking the shot. Then you stand there like a numb-nuts admiring the guy's follow-through while your man spins you and slams. We can't let people score inside against us, guys. We don't have the height, so we can't get any boards at all unless we box out *all the time*. Again!"

On and on they practiced—"Nice move, Tony. . . . Okay, Chuck, thataway to be tough. . . . Good movement, guys, keep it up. . . . No, no, no! Again!"—Pete pushing, prodding, driving them, encouraging, ragging, fretting. They ran and panted and shook their heads and growled, their sneakers squeaking on the glossy floor like a hundred mad rats. They bumped and tangled and slapped palms and soared after rebounds and ran and ran and scratched each other's arms and kicked each other's legs and swore and missed their shots and dropped their passes. They ran two beautiful plays and then two ugly ones.

"Again! . . . Again! . . . Yes! Nice feed, Mike. Good hustle! . . . No, no, no!"

Finally Pete told them to take a break.

"Tony, c'mere."

37

Tony ambled over to the sideline. "'Sup, Coach?"

"I'm worried about you, kid. You look down. You're not quick, not concentrating like I'm used to. You okay?"

"Yeah, I'm okay."

"Sure?"

"Pretty sure."

"But you're not great."

"I've had better days."

"So, what is it?"

"I'm afraid I might be flunking a course."

"Aw, what course?"

"TV."

"How can you flunk TV?"

"It's not an easy course. We don't just sit there and watch the tube, you know. All kinds of ins and outs and technical things to remember." He scuffed his toe along the sideline. "Plus I missed a few classes."

"Aw, Tony." Pete put his arm around Tony's shoulders. "Why would you do that?"

"I don't know. Personal things."

"Your girlfriend. What's her name?"

"Evonda."

"Is she . . ."

"She's okay. But she pushes, you know. Sometimes, I don't know, I just need time to think."

"Your head's gotta be straight to run this team."

"I'll be okay."

Pete slapped him on the butt and propelled him back to the team.

"Mel, find him a tutor for TV. You believe he's flunking TV? How's that possible?"

"Well, something's bugging him," the assistant coach said.

"If he's not sharp, this team comes to a grinding halt." Pete put his hands on his hips and bent forward and back, trying to ease the cranky nerves that were tying him up. The arena was stifling, even with nobody in the stands. The air was as sour as the mood. A furry movement caught the corner of his eye.

"Who let that mutt in here?"

"It's the chancellor's dog," said chubby athletic director Vic Roker, trotting heavily after the Yorkie that was flitting around among the players. "He wants to see us." He finally got ahold of a bundle of hair and hoisted the dog into his arms and came over to Pete.

"You brought the chancellor's mutt in here to see us?"

"The chancellor, Pete. Wants to see us."

"Fine. Here we are. Tell him to get his butt over here."

"That's not the way it works, Pete."

"That's how it used to work in the old days."

"Well, we're fourteen and fourteen—it's not the old days."

"You got that right. Ten minutes, I'll wrap it up."

The chancellor's office had fourteen-foot ceilings and rich mahogany paneling. Chancellor Percy Millar was tall and gawky, and had a bald pate that emerged above a circle of hair like a mountain peak jutting through the clouds. "Ah, Coach," he said, rising behind his ornate desk and leaning across to shake hands. He nodded to Vic.

"So," he said, resuming his seat as Pete and Vic sat down on the soft leather armchairs facing the desk. "Here we are. Good to see you. Yes, yes." He made a steeple of his fingers. "Tough game the other night, Pete, eh?"

"Yeah," Pete said, not returning the smile.

"Yes indeed, tough, all right. Tough."

"Let's cut to the chase, Doc," Pete said evenly. "You didn't call me in here to commiserate."

"Well, I want you to know I'm in your corner. We're behind you, yes indeed."

He opened a drawer and took out a paper napkin and handed it to Pete.

"What's this?" Pete wrinkled his nose at the *X*'s and *O*'s and arrows drawn in felt-tip on the napkin.

The chancellor cleared his throat. "It's a play. Er, a new play that I designed. Thought it might help the team. The *O*'s are offense. The *X*'s—"

"There's too many men on the court."

"Pardon?" The chancellor craned his neck to look at the napkin.

"You got six *X*'s."

The chancellor chuckled formally. "Yes, well, I haven't worked out all the details. It's the thought that counts, that sort of thing. I meant it to be kind of a trick play."

Pete raised his head and then his eyebrows.

"I call it London Bridge offense. You know. Under, over," he maneuvered his hands as if describing an aerial dogfight. "Defense falling down, that sort of thing. Just a thought."

Pete handed the napkin to Vic, who quickly scanned it and nodded.

"I see, I see," Vic said. "It's a fine play, sir."

"Why'm I here?" Pete said.

The chancellor paused. "I didn't really call you in to give you a new play." He rotated away on his chair and stared for a moment out the grand window at the rolling lawn criss-crossed by students wearing backpacks as if headed for the Himalayas. Then he turned back, leaned forward over the desk, took a gold pen out of its holder and fluttered it idly in Pete's direction.

"I called you in because we've had another bad year."

"Thanks."

"No, no, let me put it to you this way. I said 'we,' not 'you.' All of us. Me. I went to grammar school with the president of Notre Dame. We're old friends. Tease each other. He likes to call me when we lose."

"Nice touch."

"Heh-heh, well. I call him, too, of course, when *they* lose. I like that better, but they've been winning regularly. And I'm tired of his calls."

"What are you trying to say?" Pete gripped the arms of the chair.

"Easy, Coach. You're very tense. B vitamins. Decaf. As you get older, you see. The simple fact is that when we were winning championships, the alumni gave us an extra three million dollars a year. Even when we *didn't* win the national championship, if we won the conference they would still come up with an extra million in unrestricted gifts to the university."

Pete slumped back, and the air wheezed out of him, bubbling through his lips. He was so tired of the same old routine. Having to argue the same old facts, getting nowhere. He said, "The alumni are . . . well, to put it kindly, front-runners. And don't tell me about their money, if you'll forgive me, sir. We built the administration building with the eighty-four team. Your own office, this whole grand"—he waved his arm to encompass the space, meaning to say "room" but thinking "tomb," so it came out wrong— "troom, was built by three kids from Watts who were great leapers and two from the projects in Chicago who could shoot the net off the basket." Pete stood and pointed dramatically out the window, even as the chancellor was waggling his hands to calm him. "Our teams built the student union and three dormitories!"

"Petey, Pete, Coach, you've done a fine job, no question, nobody is questioning—"

" 'Done'? You saying I'm finished?" Pete sat down, mouth open, eyes narrowed.

"Not done, no, no." Millar shook his head like a dog after a swim.

"What, then?"

"Well, yes, here it is. We're not up to par. That's it. And the reason for that, it seems to me, is that we're not getting the high-quality athletes that we used to get. Not as good. Not for basketball, that is. In a nutshell."

"Of course," Roker put in gently, "our program is clean, Chancellor."

"Oh, yes, yes, to be sure, of course. Yes. Yes, but . . . you see, the football program is clean, too, of course, as you know. But they, well, win. Lately, that is."

"Jeez." Pete puffed out his cheeks. "It takes all kinds."

"Listen here." The chancellor seemed to rear up in his seat, drawing to his full seated height and tucking in his chin. "I won't—"

"Look, Doc." Pete smiled obliquely. He shifted the smile from one cheek to the other, as if sloshing a taste of wine. "See, the thing is, I don't wanna be talking out of school, Doc—he leaned forward confidentially— "but we got the inside track on the two greatest international players with amateur status."

"Really?" The chancellor leaned forward, too, and for a moment it looked as if they were both hard of hearing, the way they cocked their heads as if each waited for the other to speak.

Then Pete nodded slowly. "Blasko Rankovich from Slovenia and Teo Sakamoro from Japan. Seven feet two and seven feet four."

"A Japanese center?" The chancellor shot himself backwards, hands on the edge of the desk, arms straight.

"A board banger, sir." Pete smiled, broadly now.

"And Rankovich is even better," Roker added gingerly.

"My, my, my, my." The chancellor puckered his mouth as if about to suckle something. "I'm thrilled. This is what we've needed."

"Please, Chancellor. I've just given you very, very inside information. You've got to keep this under your hat until it's all tied up neat with letters of intent and everything. Absolutely secret."

"Absolutely." The chancellor winked and beamed.

"Now"—Pete pushed himself up and flattened his palms on his chest—"if you'll excuse me, I want to hurry back to the gym and start working on this London Bridge offense."

"Certainly, certainly. Take off. We're all finished here. Yes, you bet." He skittered around the desk to open the door.

Pete and Vic left the office and walked briskly across the campus.

Vic glanced back at the chancellor's window. "Rankovich and Sakamoro?"

"They actually exist, you know. Scientists. I saw them on the Discovery Channel about three this morning. They discovered something about tube worms. I discovered them. Added a couple feet in height and gave them a better career."

"But, Coach, he's gonna wonder."

"This'll keep him off my back until we land some real blue chippers.

"You got any leads?"

"There's the obvious guys that everybody's swarming over. I got a couple ideas of my own. But first I want to check with my Shoe Guy."

Vic chuckled and shook his head and looked down at his low-cut black and white Man-o'-Wars. "Y'know, when I coached, there was only one kind of basketball shoe. You wore it everywhere except church. And nobody paid me anything to wear them or put them on my team, let alone give them to me for free. Everything else was tennis shoes, and you wore them everywhere to do everything. Now, limousines for the feet. What a world."

"When you coached, they hadn't figured out you could cut a hole in the bottom of the peach basket."

4

THE OFFICE WAS LIKE A SNEAKER WAREHOUSE, LINED with boxes of Gazelle shoes: Man-o'-Wars, Cobras, Blue Ethers, Zephyrs, Superflies, Honeybows, Zips, Bandoliers, Yo-Mans, Hip-Hops, AK-52s, Rancheros, TruSprints. They were high-tech designs for basketball, tennis, aerobics, road racing, cross-training, hanging out. Their soles contained blended titanium dust; their arches enclosed pockets of helium; they were crisscrossed with colorful stripes and stars and swoops and angles of bright leather and polycarbonate and Velcro; they had been balanced and counterbalanced by computer; they weighed nothing and cost between $80 and $350 if you came in off the street and bought them in a store. The shoes in this office were demos and emergency stocks destined for various

46

teams and stars, and would cost them nothing. In fact, payments would be made for the privilege of providing these sneakers to the right people for lucrative display of the company's wares.

In this office was Marty Rappa, a paunchy middle-aged man with slicked-back dyed-black hair on whom suits looked like polyester no matter what they were. His shoes were Guccis spanned by gold links. He was once a salesman, then a vendor; now he was a "corporate representative" who managed the subtle deployment of these stocks of sneakers, maneuvering fiercely among the half-dozen main competitors. He recruited the best young players he could find for the company's annual summer basketball camp, where their talents would be displayed, and they in turn would display on their feet—then and in future, on whatever campus, in whatever interview, in whatever physical activity—the Gazelle logo.

Marty paced around his desk with a scowl on his face and a telephone shaped like a black and white sneaker clamped to his ear.

"Marty Rappa, Gazelle Shoes. Gimme Jake. . . . Jake? . . . Yeah, yeah. Bull. Don't bull me, Jake. You can't bull me about sneakers. One thing I know is sneakers. Yours stink. You can't get in there, so just back off. . . . Naw. Bull, he's ours. And I got the next Michael Jordan on option—nine years old and he can sky. . . . Bull!"

In the outer office Pete eyed a red-haired secretary whose desk nameplate said Gina and who had eyes like coal and legs like willow. "Hi, Gina. I'm Pete Bell, this is Mel Holly and Jack Garf, coaches from Western, to see Marty."

"You have an appointment?" she asked, smiling voluptuously.

"No, but we use his shoes."

"Right this way."

She led them through the door, and Marty, still on the phone, waved eagerly for them to sit down.

"You gonna sue me?" Marty barked into the sneaker. "Oh, yeah? I'm gonna sue you. Everybody'll sue everybody. And guess what? They'll still be wearin' our product and yours will still stink."

He slammed the phone down and immediately beamed a smile while he mopped his forehead with a white handkerchief. "Hey, guys! Good to see you. What's up?"

"You know what's up," Pete said. "I need ballplayers. Let's compare notes."

"How you guys like the Man-o'-Wars? Comfort, huh? Flashy."

"We've been working on our list," Mel said. "We listed the top one hundred blue-chip athletes in the country and reduced it to ten. Turns out they were all at your camp."

"Oh, yeah? Imagine that. You been putting down my camp for years, and suddenly all the talent is in our house. Suddenly I'm an expert."

"It's your shoes, Marty," Pete said. "We love your shoes. Been meaning to tell you. Jack, you got the list?"

"Yeah." Jack opened a folded paper. "Okay, Marty.

What do you think of Leroy Outterbridge from McClymonds High, Oakland?"

"He's committed to Southern Kentucky. Rumor says twenty-five grand changed hands."

"All right. Cornelius Brown, Central High, Marshall, Texas."

"Ho, Corny B.? Hee-hee-hee." Marty patted his stomach. "He's a head case, but he can fill it up. Anyway, rumor is, he's headed for Western Nebraska with a phony job from an alumnus congressman."

"Willie Hutcherson," Mel said, looking over Jack's shoulder. "We heard he was close to signing a letter of intent at Eastern."

"It's true. And rumor is that his old man's been driving a red Mercedes since the day Willie signed."

"Lot of rumors, huh?" Pete said, chortling.

"Yup. Lot of rumors. Same old stuff. You know how it is."

"How would we know?"

"Maybe you don't, come to think of it. Since you decided losing is the way to go. Look, guys, throw the bottom eight names away. The top two kids on your list are the only ones that matter for you. I'm sure you got 'em one-two, right?"

"Butch McRae from St. Joseph's in Chicago," Pete said, "and Ricky Roe from French Lick, Indiana."

Marty grinned and held his palms up. "Isn't it amazing how we think alike? You guys aren't so dumb as you let on. Take it from me, get those two kids and you'll go to the Final Four."

"I saw them at camp," Mel said. "They're prime, all

right. Butch could just about walk into the NBA right straight out of high school. And Ricky Roe's the next Larry Bird."

"Meaning he's white," Jack added confidentially. "How many white blue-chippers are there, after all?"

"Maybe one every decade," Marty said, "if you're lucky."

"I can feel the alumni getting excited already," Jack said.

"Hey, listen." Marty leaned over his desk on his knuckles. "I gotta tell you, these guys will be tough. You know how it works. These kids are being offered a lot of money by a lot of schools. Other stuff. The works. People are going all out."

"I don't care what everybody else is doing," Pete said. "I won championships doing things my way, and I'm still doing things my way."

"I know you don't care how other people are doing it, Pete, that's why you're losing."

"This is nutso," the cameraman said, panning the busy stage through his lens. "Looks like a carnival."

The banner at the back of the stage read: Pete Bell's Dolphin Tank. To one side, the pep band was raucously arranging itself, tuning up. Cheerleaders were stretching and hopping. Dolph the mascot was prancing back and forth, waggling his beak. At front center was a red swivel chair on which was stenciled "Hot Seat." Over the chair dangled a microphone. The stage faced an audience of students and fans in steep banks of seats, at the front of which was another microphone on a stand.

"They been doing it for years," the director said, a walkie-talkie near his ear. "Don't worry about it. You ready?"

"Anytime. They're gonna be all over the place, it looks like. Might get jumpy."

"Don't worry about it. We'll open on all the nonsense. From then on it's just Bell for you. Camera two will handle the questions. Bell is active, so be alert on tight shots. His head may suddenly duck out of frame on you. But actually we kind of like that, gives some zip to the thing."

"Weird."

"May look like that the first time around for you, but this is one of the most popular sports shows on our air."

Staff in headsets gradually organized the stage, everybody quieted, and an audible countdown came over the speakers: "Three . . . two . . . one—"

Suddenly noise erupted on and off the stage: the pep band burst into the fight song, the kids in the audience cheered and waved their arms and stomped their feet, the cheerleaders cartwheeled across the stage, followed by the mascot dolphin strutting like a drum major.

A manic cheerleader, swishing her long blond hair and flashing her long tanned thighs under her short pleated gold skirt, skipped to the Hot Seat microphone and chirped:

"Hello, Dolphins, Dolphin lovers, Dolphin symps, Dolphine Hes, and closet Dolphins everywhere. Welcome to the Dolphin Tank, with the Flagrant Fouls, our mascot Dolph the Dolphin, and Pete's Posse! And now here's the greatest coach in the universe, who's led us to nine conference titles and two national championships—the one and only Pete Bell!"

Pete had been standing in the wings trying to screw up his interest. You couldn't do a show like this without enthusiasm, any more than you could coach without it. Despite defeats, despite frustration, despite discouragement, despite repetition and boredom, despite any and all distractions and disturbances, professional or personal, major or immaterial, you had to psych yourself into positive energy. He was good at that.

He sauntered onto the stage, full of virile waves and smiles, tweaking the beak of the mascot as he passed —and drawing a honk from Dolph—and rode the cheers into the Hot Seat.

"Let's hear it for Dolph," Pete called, flinging a finger toward the mascot who responded in his dolphin suit with a bump-and-grind movement as if about to swim for the ceiling. "Without question the greatest mascot in the country!"

As the cheers and honks died, the blonde leaned into the mike. "I gotta ask you something, Coach; it was a real close game there last Friday night, real close—"

"The close ones only count in horseshoes, hand

grenades, and sometimes in the backseat of a '55 Chevy," Pete replied.

"Right, Coach. Ready for some tough questions from your fans?"

"You bet. Love the Hot Seat. Fire away. Who's first?"

A line had formed at the audience mike. The first fan, wearing a sweatshirt with a fraternity emblem on it, bumped the stand with his knee, making it quiver. "Coach Bell, why did you wait till so late to go into a zone defense the other night?"

"Not so late. I waited until the right time. We were getting beat up under the hoop. I tried different things, which maybe you didn't notice—various switches and matchups. Then the zone. Next?"

A young man with a tall flat-top Afro and wearing combat boots stepped up. "When they had sustained a sizable lead for three quarters, and you were unable to change the momentum, and they continued to be able to set up their offense at their leisure, did you consider going into an all-out press and half-court trap?"

"I considered everything. Next?"

Next was what looked to Pete like a dwarf. He seemed to have neither neck nor knees and was almost totally draped in a warm-up jacket. "Sir, as a student at this university, I would like to know if you believe in mandatory drug testing for athletes."

"No, but I believe in mandatory drug testing for students . . . starting with you. Next?"

Another student stepped up to take his shot. "Personally, I think you couldn't coach the Lakers to beat the Sisters of the Poor!"

"Hey, Sisters of the Poor are tough, but I know we can kick Our Lady of Mercy's butt."

On and on it went. To Pete it became the usual blur. None of the questioners knew what they were talking about, and the TV people appreciated his gruff and caustic answers, so he obliged them, knowing it was all a waste of time except that it was important to keep up appearances of his accessibility and forthrightness. Basically, inviting students and fans to ask him questions in front of TV cameras was like assembling a hunting party to admire a goose on a pond.

All roads led to the arena. Sidewalks streamed with people. Around the campus, flocks of students plowed out through the double doors of dormitories. Along Greek Row, massive ornate doors swung open to departing cliques of brothers and sisters in sweatshirts and denim. From all the buildings they poured, merging on the main routes to became a mighty tide of Dolphin worshipers flooding toward their shrine. Cars lined up tightly, edging their way into bloated lots. Into the shuffle and hum around the arena drifted limousines, casually disgorging movie stars, celebrities, couples dating impressively, clamorous knots of revelers who chipped in together. Chancellor Millar arrived with his retinue, Happy Kuykendall with his alumni boosters, and Slick Phil in his trench coat, skulking even in a boisterous crowd of fifteen thousand, honing his eye for an edge in his conspiratorial quest on behalf of the alumni.

It was the last game of the season, and while it did not seem a successful year to the players and coaches, as always the rite of passage was celebrated hopefully around the Western University campus; it was a social ceremony enhanced by the enduring scale and reputation of Western basketball and the attention of the internationally famous who dwelt not far from these marble halls and came to share their sporty glamour with the moiling hoi polloi and each other. It was an event.

To the players and coaches in this day and age, it was more than the last game and more than an event. It was the last opportunity to display on their home court the talent and worth that would mark their entire future. The most successful participants from this scene stood to make millions in celebrated basketball careers; the less successful would at least go out into the world of solid earnings armed with high and wide experience and college degrees. The least successful would take their mighty muscular and superbly conditioned bodies more or less home, metaphorically, to drive coal trucks.

So far they had won fourteen and lost fourteen, a record modest enough to threaten to tarnish the proud tradition of a university whose basketball team had not long ago stood at the very pinnacle of excellence as national champions, and had not lost more games than it had won in any season of this generation. And these boys had all come from successful high school programs into this one, and not one of this squad had ever experienced a losing season in his entire athletic life. So a lot was riding on this final game of a so-so season, against Coast University.

In the locker room, Western's players sprawled on benches trying to relax, some leaning back with arms folded and legs stretched out and crossed, some hunched forward leaning on their knees, staring at their Man-o'-Wars, fidgeting with their fingers laced. Some chewed gum, some their nails; some licked their lips, feeling dry mouths.

"This is the last game of this season," Coach Bell said, as he paced around the locker room. "For some of you it is the last game of your college careers. For some of you it is the last game of your lives. We've won just half our games. Tonight determines whether we finish above or below five hundred—whether we have a winning season or a losing one."

This was a time for focusing, and one of the crucial skills of a coach was his ability not just to inspire, not just to teach, but at the proper moments of engagement to cause his players to focus on exactly what their immediate jobs were. A focus tighter than they were used to, finer than they had thought possible a few weeks before. Pete had spent a lot of years pounding into himself the ability to focus.

"Winning is not something to celebrate. Winning is the way it's supposed to be. Losing is a mistake, an aberration. We will win the game tonight with our defense," he said in a chanting cadence. "Our defense is our offense. We look like matadors out there. Olé, olé, olé! Wave 'em through! There's the basket, fellas, come on in! No! The defense can dictate the tempo of the game if the team playing defense has heart! Does anybody here know what a heart is? Do you?"

He went to the blackboard, picked up a piece of chalk, and savagely slashed out a vaguely familiar shape.

"What's that?" he barked, suddenly raising his voice. "Say it! I want to hear voices!"

"Heart . . . A heart . . . That's a heart. . . ."

"It's a heart, that's what it is. And if you show me you got one then we'll win this game tonight! Tony, you got one of these?"

"Yes, sir," said the point guard, handling a basketball as usual, running his hands continually over it as if molding a clay sphere.

"Do you understand our defensive philosophy and how it triggers our transition game?"

"Yessir."

"Do you think the entire team understands this philosophy of execution and transition?"

"Yessir."

The other players nodded and muttered.

"Good. Because I'm holding you responsible, Tony, for the complete team understanding of this philosophy. You accept that responsibility?"

"Yessir."

"Okay." He nodded around sternly at the players, trying to meet their eyes. "Okay. Because out there on the court is where you have the heart. It doesn't come from the school or from me, not when you're out there. You're on your own. The heart is in you. And Tony, I'm also holding you responsible for this entire team's demonstration that it has a heart!"

"Yes, sir."

Abruptly he hollered: "We must win this game! We will not have the first losing season in forty years at this university!"

But it was not to be. The tone was set early when the quick Coast guards penetrated almost at will. Pete called a couple of early time-outs to settle the Dolphins down.

"We're okay, we're okay," he told them. "We just gotta tighten up the D. Tony, we gotta be patient on the offense. When they come running at us and score, that doesn't mean we have to fire back and put it up right away. Calm down now on offense, step it up on defense. We can't take our eyes off those guards for an instant, not even after they pass off. They're still hot, they cut, they're fast. Stay with them. Don't get discouraged. They can't run like this all night."

But Coast continued to run. Tony hurried a three-pointer that clanked off the back of the rim and was rebounded by a Coast forward who triggered a quick outlet pass to one of their guards, and Coastal shot out on a fast break that ended with a trailing forward scoring on a slam dunk.

"We don't run the play," Pete said to Mel. "We throw up a low-percentage shot, we don't box out on the boards, and then we don't get back on defense. Four mistakes in eight seconds!"

Mel just nodded.

At halftime, the Dolphins trailed by ten.

"Not too bad," Pete told them in the locker room, "considering how many mental mistakes we've made. In fact, given how bad we've played, we're in great shape. We are still in this game. Tony, things are holding up pretty good, the plays have smoothed out, we're more patient. Rafe," he said to the other guard, a quiet and dependable senior with no hopes of pro ball, "you've got to put it up more. They're dropping off you because they don't think you'll shoot. We have to take those shots. Chuck," he turned to the tired center, "I know you've got your hands full with those guards cutting by you all the time, but you've got to push your man out. He's ending up too close to the boards. Keep pushing him out until they call a couple of fouls on you."

He tried to rally them in a low-key way, trying not to transmit to them his discouragement. They knew the stakes. They were being outplayed not because of their mental mistakes but because they didn't have the size and speed and shooting skill they needed. He could only make them work harder.

In the second half they made a couple of brief runs, Tony beginning to take things into his own hands, driving, hitting jumpers, going for steals. They cut the lead down to four, then sank again. Coastal hit the last three shots to win by twelve.

"Hold your heads up, guys!" Pete barked at them as he stomped among the benches in the locker room. "We did a lot of good things out there tonight, lot of positive things."

The fagged players sagged on the benches, the sweat continuing to drain from them, slickening the benches and floor mats. Their feet were red when they pulled off their socks; their arms bore red and blue blotches from banging their opponents; here and there on some of them were red scratches. It was that way after every game, but after the losses they felt the hurts sooner as their bodies cooled.

"We worked hard," Pete went on. "We never quit."

"Shoulda worked harder," came a mutter. "Didn't hit the boards. Shoulda left pieces of ourselves out there . . . not good enough." Other mutters echoed around the room.

"All right, all right. It's over. We did what we could. Can't change it. Get your heads up. Seniors, I thank you for your effort for four years. Finish up strong and get your degrees, and I hope you continue to support the program."

He meandered around. The players sighed and slowly pulled off their uniforms.

"Listen, the papers will bad-mouth us tomorrow. Don't worry about it. Just remember, they don't know anything. They don't know what went on, how hard we worked in practices, what we were trying to do. They don't know the *game*. What matters is what we think of ourselves."

He folded his arms and studied the drooping boys. Tony's face was buried in his hands.

"Tony, get your head up! You're a leader on this team, and you've got another season left with us, and I'm counting on you."

He resumed his striding, more purposefully now, because he wanted to wrap this scene up. "Listen, everybody. When you walk out of this arena, you always walk out with your heads high. Nobody should be able to tell whether you won or lost from the way you carry yourselves. If you're giddy with laughter when you win, it sends the world a message that you're not used to winning. If your head is high when you lose, it tells the world that this loss was an aberration. It tells the world you will win tomorrow. This loss was not a disgrace—it was a mistake. You haven't done anything wrong. None of the people who will criticize you have worked as hard as you guys, and none of them ever played basketball better than you."

Suddenly he turned and slammed his palm against a locker. "It doesn't matter what the record says. We are winners!"

Then he stomped out and down the cold corridor toward the exit.

5

WE AREN'T WINNERS, WE'RE LOSERS," PETE GROWLED. "No matter how you slice it, we ain't playing with a whole loaf. We are a staggeringly mediocre basketball team."

His three assistant coaches slumped wearily in Pete's office, winding down from the game and the season, none of them anticipating with pleasure this debriefing or what their losing season might portend for their jobs. They all figured that as long as Pete stayed, they would stay. You don't fire the assistants and keep the head coach. But Pete's future was not immediately clear.

"They're a great bunch of kids," Jack said hopefully.

"Best kids I ever had! Gonna be pillars of the community. So what? Not one of them can play basketball good enough for us to win at this level. Except Tony, and he's flunking TV."

"I got him a tutor," Mel said softly. "He'll be okay."

"He's something we can build around," Jack Garf said, pursing his lips and nodding thoughtfully, "like a nucleus. You know what I mean? When you've got a good point guard to run the team on the floor. So we can build around him." He molded air with his hands.

"Terrific," Pete said. "All we need is four other starters and a bench."

"I didn't mean to minimize—"

"I have never learned to lose!" Pete said, jumping up and starting to pace, staring at the floor, his hands jammed into his pockets. "The day I make peace with losing is the day I walk away from this business. Winning is expected! Winning is the norm! Winning is how it's supposed to be! Everything else is an aberration!" He stalked back and forth, working his lips. "Five years ago we were national champions. And now look at us. Who would have believed we could sink this fast?"

"We'll win again," Mel said.

"We don't have ten years here!" Pete barked. "We don't have five. We don't have *two* years to show something. Nobody gives you any time anymore. TV money is too big. Everything is bim, bam, bing. Mediocre don't cut it. Good citizenship don't cut it. Cooperative don't cut it."

"Nice guy don't cut it," Jack offered.

"So what has happened here? Do I stink?"

"Lot of players started going east," Mel said, "because TV exposure got so big so fast out there."

"TV exposure got big everywhere. I think we stopped working hard enough. We were champions. We sat on our hands and waited for athletes to come to us, like they used to. We didn't get out there and beat the bushes for the talent."

"I feel like we worked pretty hard," Freddie said.

"Yeah? Either I stink as a coach, we all stink as coaches, or we didn't get the athletes. Which is it? Huh?"

"We could have used more height," Freddie said.

"I'll say. Man, we let that seven-foot Jones kid slip away—right out of our own neighborhood!"

"He got a bag of money to go east," Jack said. "That's what I heard. Maybe that's what it takes."

Pete fixed his eyes on Jack. "To do what?"

"Well"—Jack shrugged—"to get 'em to come here. I mean, maybe eventually we have to ante up like everybody else."

"Knock it off. What everybody else did or didn't had nothing to do with us winning championships. Now, let's get some imagination going here. Who's out there in junior colleges right now?"

"Junior colleges?" Freddie furrowed his brow. "I thought you didn't like working with those JC guys, all those transfer types."

"I didn't think I'd ever have a fourteen-and-fifteen season, either. Maybe we gotta try some new routes."

"Maybe we gotta go after Butch McRae and Ricky Roe," Mel said quietly.

But Pete didn't seem to hear. He was stalking around the room muttering: "I can't even say fourteen and fifteen. Those words don't make sense coming out of my mouth. It's wacky. Upside down. I can't believe it. Nobody believes it. I don't even want to think about it. . . ."

And, still muttering and shaking his head, he left the room.

"Beat it, mister. You know the rules."

"But, Tony," Axelby said, trying to keep up the pace walking beside him, "I'm not asking you for an interview. Just a reaction. Just how you're feeling."

"Hey." Tony stopped abruptly and turned to lock eyes with his pursuer. "Just how I'm feeling is just my business and nobody else's. Plus, any time you want to talk to players, you're supposed to clear it through Coach Bell. Everybody knows that."

"With other teams, we go through the public information office."

"I don't know about other teams."

"It's impossible to go through Coach Bell."

"I'm outta here."

"All I want is just to compare how you felt after the season two years ago, compared to this. Because there was some trouble, some, uh, distractions, rumors, right or wrong. I mean, you're an articulate, thoughtful kid. Honest kid, right?"

Tony was already trotting off into the night, gritting his teeth.

Axelby gritted his teeth too, ground them, standing there rubbing his chin as Tony disappeared in the dark. "Everybody lies," Axelby mumbled. "That's the trouble with this world. You can't trust anybody. Everybody's dirty, stinking, lousy. Everybody runs. Everybody deserts. . . ."

A few minutes later he was ringing a familiar doorbell.

"Mr. Axelby, you're wasting your time."

"Please, Mrs. Bell, I just want—"

"I'm not Mrs. anything." Jenny stood in the doorway, gritting her teeth, trying to remain pleasant.

"Sorry. I just . . . well, I want to clear up a possible misunderstanding."

"Misunderstanding? How could there be a misunderstanding? I haven't told you anything. Not now, not before. I'm not a part of any of this."

"But you see, um, I wanted to make sure that you didn't . . . You see, I have been trying to talk to you about a purely professional matter."

"I understand. I just have nothing to say."

"But there may be somebody who misunderstands why I have tried to talk to you. Somebody might even think it was *personal,* for heaven's sake."

"I barely know your name. How in blazes could it be personal? I think I'm beginning to get annoyed."

"Please," Ed Axelby began talking fast, "just a profile of Coach Bell, how he's holding up through crises, kind of guy, background . . ."

"I'm now going to make this personal, Mr. Axelby. You have no business here. Plus I have discovered that I don't like you. Plus I don't trust you. Plus if you show up here again, I will call your newspaper and say that you are harassing me. Plus I will tell Pete Bell. No misunderstanding now, is there?"

Ed Axelby stood staring at the closed door, hoping that no one in the world would ever find out about this mistake. But Bell didn't like him anyway and wouldn't talk to him, so who cares. He walked off toward his car, whistling lightly. She was a looker, all right. If you liked shrews. No wonder Coach Bell left her. But Bell wasn't going to get away with any secrecy. Big-time athletic programs were dirty. Bell always presented himself as so holy and pure. Axelby didn't mind so much that programs were dirty—a fact of life. He didn't mind so much that coaches and A.D.s lied about it—another of life's slimy little facts. But he *did* mind that Bell wouldn't talk to him, let his hair down, let Axelby in on the secrets behind the scenes, wouldn't let his players talk to him.

Ed Axelby was used to being an insider, having that smug knowledge of the privileged. He resented being left out.

The man Pete Bell always referred to as slick Phil—Phil Driller—hung up his trench coat and sat down in the smoky room with Happy Kuykendall and several of Happy's alumni shakers. Phil was not technically an alumnus. He was in fact a freelance snooper. He sold his information, sometimes to the highest bidder, sometimes to people he just liked. He had a couple of fine-tuned instincts. One was his uncanny sense of just where he would be most appreciated and when. The other was that he knew just how much information to reveal and what to keep to himself. He was quite capable of playing one person against another, even within the same bunch, and without anyone realizing it. He was a true independent. Sometimes he just liked to have fun with his talent for sniffing things out. Lately he had been having a good time around Happy and the boys at Western.

Happy dealt.

"One-eyed jacks wild," Happy said. "So what'd you find out for us, Phil, anything?"

"I think he's gonna go after A and B," Phil said out of the corner of his mouth. "You know who I mean. He's gonna run into a wall. You got the chancellor. He'll be there when we need him. We got Bell in a corner, so we can just let him make his trips and get interested. Then when he hits the wall we'll be his only way out. Axelby has done plenty of sniffing around. But Bell has never budged, never given him anything. So we're safe there. Whatever Bell does will be private. Including us, of course. But nobody else will have a clue. He'll cooperate. Two cards."

Happy flipped him two cards. "You don't think Pete's close to going off the deep end, do you?"

"Naw. He's tough. When push comes to shove, he wants to win just like everybody else. He doesn't want anything else for himself. He'll come around."

"I heard something about some Japanese guy named Leo or Theo or something," one of the men said, shifting his cigar in his mouth and studying his cards, "and some Slovenian named Rankovich— couple huge hot guys he may have an in to. That who you're talking about?"

"Oh, come on, Joe," Phil said. "That's just a jive smoke screen. You don't think I'd know about these guys? They don't exist. Bell's just trying to tap-dance while he figures out what the real world's all about. What'sa matter with your head? You wanna know what's going on, ask me."

Five dollars was tossed into the pot. The others added theirs.

Happy rubbed his chin. "We're doing what's right," he said. "All we're trying to do is bring Pete Bell into this century. It's time we stood up and brought our special talents to bear."

"Yeah," Phil said. "You got as much right to win as Indiana or North Carolina or anybody else. God don't like losers."

A totally empty arena was like a mausoleum, Pete always thought. Eerie and ominous, discouraging to visitors. Pete sat in the first row of seats and gazed into the vast space, the soaring tiers of seats, the massive spanning beams, the still banners hanging overhead. The glistening floor on which the game was played seemed not to belong in this silent scene; it should be earth and swords. He sat there listening to his breathing echo amid the creaks of the building.

"What're you doing here?"

Pete turned to see Vic Roker emerge from an aisle. "Me? What's an A.D. doing here at two o'clock in the morning?"

"Just wandering. Couldn't sleep. You?"

"I don't know. Kind of peaceful, I guess, being in this place without worrying about the score."

Vic sat down beside him, and they both leaned on their knees and stared at the floor.

"Doesn't look like you're about to start enjoying the off-season," Vic said.

Pete chuckled. "There isn't any off-season, not anymore."

"Nope. Too bad. Seasons get longer, it all gets harder."

"This season sure was long."

"Maybe we should just retire."

"You retire, you old fart."

"Not so long as I've got to watch over you. What're you thinking about?"

"Oh, history. Other teams used to come in here and see our championship banners hanging up there and they were intimidated from the git-go."

"I used to figure those banners were worth eight points a game."

"Twelve points a game. Easy."

"Oh, well, this season's bygones. Maybe next year we'll . . ." Vic's voice drifted off.

"We'll what? Win? Yeah. Everything changes."

"Everything changes."

"Am I overcoaching?" Pete looked at Vic. "Am I keeping them on too tight a rein?"

"Naw, not a chance, Pete. These guys needed every bit of direction you could give them. You just couldn't *play* for them is all."

"We had a small front line. But so did Wooden in 'sixty-two."

"So did *you,* in 'eighty-two. They were even smaller than this line."

"Everybody was smaller a decade ago."

"Even me."

"Yeah, you moose." Pete playfully slapped Vic's head. "You better lose some flab around your heart."

"I think I'm just getting shorter."

Pete got up and started to pace back and forth. "It's getting impossible to keep up with the world. I mean, I'm trying to figure . . . the commies went down in one big flush. All the Reds in the universe turn out to be wimps. Who'da thought?"

"Not me. Amazing."

"Unbelievable. Michael Jordan quits. Everything is wacky."

"What are you talking about?"

"People are dying of a disease that we didn't even know about fifteen years ago. Ozone's got a hole in it. I don't even know what ozone is and now it has a hole in it that's bad news."

Vic eyed Pete, whose teeth and hands were

clenched. "What's the point, Pete? What's eating at you?"

"Here's the point." Pete stopped pacing and turned abruptly to face him. "There's very little going on in the world that anybody has any real control over. Things happen. You can plan your head off, doesn't matter. Things just happen the way they happen. Good things, bad things. You got to grab it when you can. Just be alert at all times and grab." Pete made grabbing motions in the air.

"Grab what, exactly?"

"If you want to make a statement, you got to *make* it. No pussyfooting. Bim, bam, bang."

"You want to make a statement?"

"Of course. We *all* want to make a statement. Whatever it is. I haven't been making a statement lately."

"What you wanna say?"

"When we were winning conference titles and going to the Final Four every year, we were making a statement. We were saying, 'Here we are, that's *who* we are.' You get some control. You grab it. Everything is better."

"Lots of things were better when we were younger," Vic said.

"No, not younger, you dimwit. When we were making a *statement*. It's only when we lose that edge, get tired, give up, relax—when we stop making a statement is when we get old and shrivel up and die."

"Whew!" Vic stared at him, wide-eyed. "You sure are wound up."

Pete resumed pacing. "Vic, the banners don't win for us anymore. We need players. I need talent, athletes, horses. I'm coaching as good as I know how, and that isn't good enough anymore. We've got to have the horses."

"Thoroughbreds."

"But half the coaches in the country are *buying* these high school players!" Pete thumped a fist into his palm. "Money under the table, cars, girls, whatever. And we all know it."

"Yup." Vic nodded, relieved to have Pete back on the subject of basketball, at least.

"It's illegal, it's unethical, it's immoral, it's—"

"Pete, calm down." Vic waggled his hands. "Nobody said you had to cheat. Winning runs in cycles. It'll come around again."

"Bull!" Pete swatted Vic's hands. "I ain't no Maytag. You know that's bull. Don't patronize me. We can't sit here waiting for a cycle. We have to get control. However." Pete stopped and chewed his lip for a moment. "There's two reasons I'm incapable of cheating. One—if I break the rules I might get busted and thrown out of coaching for the rest of my life, and that means I won't be drawing X's and O's for a buncha kids I love, teaching 'em how to work together even if they hate each other 'cause who else are they gonna have for a mother when they're here. The fact is that all the bull of alumni and agents and shoe contracts and reporters is worth it if I teach these kids how to play basketball and, just a little bit, how to become men." He paused. "I could lose all the rest."

Vic waited. Pete seemed caught up in a thought. "What's the second reason, Pete?"

Pete stared at him. "I might *not* get caught."

6

HEY, TIGER. 'SUP?"

"Coach, I was wondering. Maybe we could get together and talk for a few minutes."

"Sure, Tony. Wanna come over?"

"Well . . ."

"Tell you what. Let's meet over at Devon. I can feed you for some hoops, get a close look at your motion. We can talk."

"Great."

"Half hour. See you there."

Devon Playground was commonly deserted in the early evening. There was nothing unusual about talking to Tony, but it was always easier if he could be doing something. Tony wasn't so comfortable facing you in a chair or across a table.

He was waiting when Pete got there, sitting on the asphalt ground, leaning back against the chain-link fence and molding a basketball in his hands. He bounced the ball to Pete and walked onto the court. He was wearing knee-length black shorts and a plain white T-shirt. Twilight was dimming quickly.

Pete began feeding him passes as Tony moved around the perimeter, shooting jumpers from twelve to twenty feet. He received the ball and jumped in a fluid motion, head up, releasing the ball quickly and giving it a slow, precise backward spin. The percentage that hit the net was not high—Tony was not primarily a shooter. But he was strong and wiry and smooth now, at six feet four, and he could carry more weight easily; his passing and playmaking were excellent, his court sense fine, his work ethic and reliability first rate. Pete was sure that his shooting would improve next season; he could become a shooter. And he had everything else. He was a terrific kid, always had been, right out of the Chicago projects. He had a future.

Pete just let him shoot for a while.

"Coach," Tony said, taking a break to catch his breath, "I was wondering." He stared off. "What if I didn't try to play pro ball?"

Pete studied him. "Why wouldn't you want to play pro?"

Tony shrugged. "I don't know. Been playing ball all my life. Maybe I'm getting tired of it."

"We had a rough season. Don't let that get to you. You got one more year here, and you'll shoot more.

You'll get stronger. Why're you thinking about it now?"

He shrugged again. "Thinking maybe I should be making decisions. For my future, you know? Basketball's risky. May not make it. May not like it."

"Not *like* it? Tony, what's going on?"

"Life, I guess."

"Your old lady?"

"Not really. She's not really my old lady. We're just kinda close. But no, it's not her. Not exactly. I mean, some of the things we talk about kind of brought it up. About what kind of person I am. What kind I want to be."

"You're a super person."

"That Axelby's been trying to talk to me."

"What?"

"I told him to get out of my face. Don't worry about it. Don't say anything, okay? I can handle him. He ain't nothing."

"Okay. What else?"

"I been thinking. Maybe I just rather get a job, you know, nine to five, wear a tie. Have a home, get a dog. You know, just ordinary stuff."

"You're not leaving school." Pete narrowed his eyes.

"Well, I was thinking about it. Maybe just getting my degree at night, something like that." Tony didn't look at him.

"You're not leaving school. You're not leaving the team. So you can forget that. Whatever it is that's bugging you, we'll work it out."

Tony was silent. He took a deep breath and chewed his lip.

"Look." Pete put a hand on his shoulder. "You want to talk, you know I will talk to you anytime, about anything. Now, later . . . I don't know what's happened to you about basketball, but I want you to get away from it for a while. I don't want you to touch a basketball for a month. Okay?"

"Maybe that's all it is, just need to get away from it."

"Let's go home."

Pete wearily unlocked the door and shuffled into his house. He dragged himself straight to the bedroom and flopped down on the bed. Just a couple of beers at Shakey's had seemed to knock him out. There had been a time when he could knock back boilermakers all night and still play Ping-Pong. Now, well, things had changed.

Not that he wanted to drink like the old days. He just wanted to be *able* to drink.

It wasn't even late. Midnight, not late enough. He wished the night was over. He wished it was summer. He wished the students were gone. The NCSA tournament was in full swing, and for the second straight year he wasn't even in it. The National Collegiate Sports Association was a bunch of old fart white hypocrites. They needed a whole housecleaning over there, if college athletics were to get straightened out. They had allowed all the under-the-table stuff to grow to this outrageous, open flagrancy that everyone was talking about. They were afraid to crack down on anybody, at least any of the big-shot campuses. So it went on. The NCSA was out of date and out of touch and out of gas.

But the NCSA was all there was. The NCSA was college sports. The basketball tournament that led to the Final Four and the championship was theirs. It was the best thing they did, put on that national tournament. Sixty-four teams. Not including Western University. Not for two years.

Unbelievable. He swung his legs off the bed, took a recent game tape from the pile, put it in the VCR, and lay back with the remote control. He tried to study the game, pick out flaws, come up with ideas, learn, decide. . . .

"Yeech!" He popped out the tape and flung it against the wall and turned on CNN to watch the news.

Until then he had ignored the flashing light on his telephone-answering machine. There was nobody he wanted to talk to or hear from just now. But he reached over and tapped the button and lay back as Jenny's throaty, sexy voice came on.

"Hi, Pete. Me. You there? Yes, no? I saw the game. You did a great coaching job—you just don't have the players. Don't read the papers—you're doing great. Pete? You there? I want to see you. Right now. I'll come over. Pete, when I'm not remembering what a miserable jerk you were to be married to, I miss you a lot. So, uh, well, give me a call, okay? Sometime. 'Bye.''

Pete bubbled his lips and closed his eyes. It had been so tough to get used to the split. How could he get over her when she called like that? What a crock. Just like a woman.

"Please," he roared at the ceiling. "Leave me alone!"

If he hadn't stopped at Shakey's, he would've been home by nine. He felt as if the fates were toying with him. His toothache returned; he wondered if it was psychosomatic. He had to get his life under direction. He had to make a statement. He couldn't wait. He had to attack. Had to grab for it.

When they came down out of the clouds, the world was white. Chicago was covered with a spring snow. The jets on the runways at O'Hare churned up blinding ground clouds. It was a jolt that took him back to his roots in Iowa.

He had almost forgotten that he'd played basketball in the winter, when it snowed. All his childhood associations with basketball had to do with football ending in the nick of time, when sitting in the stands at the last football game was risking frostbite. Basketball meant getting indoors, entering the locker room through a narrow gap in the snowdrift, working up a heavy sweat on the court, then bucking back outside against the wind and temperatures that felt refreshing for a little while.

BLUE CHIPS

In those days when a kid was over six feet tall he played on the front line. Pete had been a rugged six-foot-one-inch forward. Today they would call a guy a "power forward" as opposed to "small forward" if his main talent and responsibility were, as were Pete's, crashing the boards and making bodies roll, but back then there was no distinction. You were left or right forward, and forwards were the guys who were taller than the guards and shorter than the center. Pete had been in demand for football too, as a fullback, but he was a borderline student and had to choose one sport or the other.

He loved the patterns of basketball. He was not so much recognized for that, and for a long time didn't notice it himself, because he was such a banger. Teammates treated him like a leader—he was senior captain—because of his hard work. But by his senior year he had become a student of the game. Much as he loved to play, he loved watching it just as much, and figuring out movements and strategy, doping out tactics and plays, spotting talent, predicting the course of a game.

His high school teams had not been great—12–8 his last year—and he was not an all-star. He was just a solid, smart workhorse.

He drove himself hard in basketball. His family raised hogs, and he preferred the hard court to the family business, and his teammates to his gruff and silent and dreary parents, so basketball had been his ticket off the farm.

In college he made the freshman team and sat on the bench; he didn't quite make the varsity, but by then the coaches had noticed his basketball brains. He became a part-time assistant coach. His career was launched, even as a student.

After graduation he stayed on as regular assistant for a couple of years, then went on to Pennsylvania and Arizona, prepping for the big jobs. He became head coach at the smaller Lake Michigan College and led the Oremen to three big winning seasons. That broke him out. He was hired away by Western University.

His mother died of pneumonia, and soon after that his father went with a stroke. What was left for Pete was basketball, a marriage headed for the rocks, and more basketball. His life was totally devoted to basketball. There was no time for anything else. Winning had made it all worthwhile.

Now in Chicago, looking for a winner, he rented a Taurus and headed for the inner city.

Two hours later, after a coffee and honey bun at a luncheonette, he maneuvered his way through a dimly lit public housing project and pulled up outside a stolid gray stone edifice across whose front was sculpted a name: Saint Joseph's High School.

There were only a few stragglers along the street. When Pete stepped out of the car he knew why: a bitter wind lashed his face. He hurried into the building and followed his ears to the gym.

The place was packed to the rafters and roaring. A

quick glance at the scoreboard—SJ Cavs 35; Carmel 19—a scan of the seats to find the familiar faces, and Pete climbed up the aisle to join the bunch of college coaches and scouts with their notebooks.

"Hey, Busher," Pete said, settling in next to a man whose bald brown pate glistened in the lights. "Can he play?"

"Hey, Pete." Busher Lee grabbed his hand. "Now *all* the big guns are here. You ask, can he play? Lookit him. He moves like a cat."

Butch McRae reversed his dribble, spun, and hung in the air for a five-foot bank shot, drawing gasps, headshakes, and cheers from the home crowd, and nods from the scouts.

"Can he *play!* There it is. This is the fourth game I've seen. And he's as happy with an assist as with a bucket."

McRae took an outlet pass and drove the court for a dunk.

"Wow." Pete gave a low whistle. "You got a chance at him?"

"You might say." Busher chuckled and leaned over to whisper hoarsely in Pete's ear. "We recruited his girlfriend."

"Get out!"

"Truth." Busher held up a palm as if he were taking an oath.

"That's all?"

"That's enough, generally."

McRae gave a ball fake that sent his defender

stumbling backwards, and drilled a smooth twenty-footer. Then he stole the inbounds pass and passed behind his back to his center, who jammed.

"Well, maybe generally. But Father Dawkins runs this place like General Patton. He'll have a lot to say about it."

"Ain't Father Dawkins I'm worried about. It's Butch's mama that calls the shots. And she calls 'em by some names new even to me."

"I heard she's a killer."

"Chew you *and* spit you out. She wants a grand just to talk."

"I don't pay money to talk to anybody's mother," said Pete.

"Even his mother?" taunted Busher.

"You give her a grand?" Pete asked.

"Yo, Pete, you don't ask me that. Anyway, I haven't talked to her. Not yet. By the way," Busher ran his hand over his bald head, "what's going on with your program out there?"

"Don't ask. It's been rough. I miss having you around."

"We ran it up a few times at Lake Michigan, didn't we?"

"You're still running it up in Carolina."

"Sometimes. You'll get back."

"You know how it works, Busher."

Butch McRae led the fast break, took a return pass, slipped the ball behind his back, and floated in for a layup.

"Wow!" Pete and Busher said together.

Pete slipped out of his seat and through the bunch of coaches, tapping some on the back, shaking hands, waving, and went down under the bleachers to the corner of the gym where he had seen Jake.

Jake was the grandfather of one of Pete's players at Lake Michigan—served actually as the boy's father because the real one had disappeared—and had been a devoted and involved mentor to the kid. Jake had aged a lot since Pete had last seen him, his curly hair gone all white. In his janitor's coveralls, Jake leaned on the push broom he would use to sweep the court at halftime.

"It's always good to see you, Coach Bell, yes, indeed," Jake said, holding out his hand. "I hope you're well."

"How you been, Jake? How's the boy?"

"I'm just fine. And the boy, he's just fine, too, Coach Bell. His little business coming along. Two sweet little kids of his own."

"He helping you out?"

"Well, now, I won't allow that. You know me, I got my ways. Anyways, I'm fine."

Pete turned to face the court. "You know this McRae kid?"

"Sure."

"I see he can play. But what kind of kid is he?"

"Most solid kid I ever seen go through here, Coach Bell. That's a fact."

"Okay. That's important, coming from you." Pete gripped his arm with one hand and locked hands with the other. *"You're* important, Jake. Don't forget that."

"And that means a lot to me, coming from you, Coach. Thank you. Good luck, hope you get him."

Pete strode into the lounge outside the principal's office, greeting the seated gathering of the same coaches and scouts he had seen at the game.

"Hey, Pete . . . look who's here. . . . Long ways from home. . . . Put on a little weight. . . . Didn't you used to be a coach somewhere? . . . look out, the shark is here. . . . Wish I had your expense account. . . ."

Pete nodded, chuckled, shook hands here and there. "You guys must all be here looking for Rhodes Scholars, right?"

"Rhodes Scholars that can dunk," spouted one of the coaches.

"Yeah, we heard they got a lot of good students," said another. "Must be why *you're* here."

Pete went straight through the room to the secretary's desk. "Pete Bell, Western University." She nodded and entered his name on a list. Pete looked around. "Why don't you tell Father Dawkins I'm here"—he leaned forward conspiratorially—"and send these other clowns home."

She lifted her phone as Pete wandered back among the coaches to exchange small talk.

Less than a minute had passed when the principal's door swung open, and through it strolled a tall and muscular black Catholic priest with his clerical collar undone and dangling over his black shirt. He smiled broadly, a caricature, and sashayed around the room with his arms spread as if to envelop this odd flock.

"Well, my, my, my," he intoned theatrically, "if it ain't some powerhouse representatives of the wide and scholarly world in covetous assembly." He tipped his head back and put his palms together reverently. "There is blood in the water, I do declare! And the odor wafteth far and deep, summoning *all* the beasts of the oceans."

There were chortles around the room from those who knew him, wary sidelong glances from those who hadn't been exposed to him before.

"Now, what have we here?" He deepened his voice and tucked in his chin and thrust out his lips. "Must be a big point guard on the block! That must be it! Then step up and start the bidding. Who'll give me fifty dollah for this strapping young boy, sebenteen yeahs ole and growin' ever day? Dig down, mah frens, way down into them promisin' pockets where the future is, because we talkin' 'bout a lad what can both read *and* write, yassah! Ain't no Abdul Mohammad sass. Boy got the name of Butch. That's a name callin' up *freckles*. Yas, yas, my, my, dig deep, my frens, 'cause you got to come up with a bundle!"

There was silence as the recruiters eyed each other nervously, but Pete laughed out loud at this performance.

Father Dawkins stood with his hands on his hips, suddenly looking stern and forbidding. "I can only hope you aren't all outright jackals," he said. "Pete, good to see you. Come on in."

He disappeared back into his office, and Pete followed, and groans and sighs and growls and hissed curses followed him as he shut the door.

Father Dawkins tipped back in his swivel chair and put his feet up on his cluttered desk.

"Still smoking those Gauloise stinkers, huh, chief?" Pete said.

Dawkins chuckled and tapped the ashes off his cigarette. "'Fraid so. Ever since 'Nam. By the way, you're still the only one around that knows I'm half Cherokee. Got to keep that quiet."

"Indians are *in*, Chief, these days."

"Not in *my* neighborhood. So, let's get down to business. Most important things first. How's Tony?"

"He's fine. Struggling some with school. A little burnt out with basketball, I think."

"Struggling? Is he going to class?"

"He's trying. He's okay. I'm not worried about him. He works hard for me."

"I love him and always will, Pete. But if he flunks, that's his own lookout. Don't baby him. Basketball's only *part* of it."

"There's two kinds of athletes in the world: the kind that need pats on the head and the kind that need kicks in the butt. Tony's very responsive to the latter educational philosophy."

"Well, I know you're attentive, keep an eye on your kids. That's why I'm glad he's out there with you. Now, second most important, how are you?"

"I'm fine, too. Well, I'm okay. Rough season. Learning how to be a bachelor again. Normal stuff."

"Heh-heh. Most men don't learn how to *be* men till their women go away. You're here about Butch McRae, of course."

"He's something, eh?"

"Best we've ever had. And he's smart. Head's screwed on right. Doesn't make mistakes. You see him following Tony?"

"I can actually see him playing *with* Tony. Tony's gonna be a shooter next year. He can play either spot."

"What a backcourt."

"How about his mama?"

"You've heard, I gather. Well, she's a powerful piece of work. Personally, I like her. Nothing slips by her. And she'll die for Butch, you better believe."

"I'd like to talk to her but I heard she wants dough just to talk."

"Oh, she'll stick it to reps or schools she doesn't like. But I think it's like this: she's put her life into Butch; now, when she sends him on his way, she may feel she deserves a little comfort and security in her old age."

"Does she like us?"

"She likes your science department"—Dawkins put his feet down, lit another Gauloise, and rested on his elbows—"better than your basketball program."

"Science department's probably got a better record than we have lately."

"Look, Pete, I'll put in a word for you, and that'll get you past the toll booth. But I've gotta warn you: She knows what's up. You try foolin' with Lavada McRae, she'll eat you alive."

"Would I?"

"Naw. I figure your job's on the line pretty soon. You're too good a guy, too good a coach, to get bounced. So you'll be smart. I wouldn't call her for you otherwise."

"Great. Praise the Lord for me, will you, Chief?"

"Praise him yourself, honky." Father Dawkins stood up and reached across the desk to shake hands. "I'll get back to you today. Don't mention anything to those other guys out there, okay?"

"You're one safe Cherokee with me, Chief."

7

HE THOUGHT ABOUT IT FOR QUITE A WHILE, THEN decided, why not. He called Jenny.

"I got your message," he said, "and I appreciate it. Just didn't have a chance to call."

"Want to come over?"

"I'm in Chicago. Recruiting trip."

"You waited until you were in Chicago to call me?"

"I didn't *wait* until I was in Chicago. It just happened."

"Oh, well, that's okay. The mood has passed anyway."

"Don't say that."

"You always get lonely when you're in a hotel room. I'll talk to you when you get back."

He drove into a neighborhood of run-down buildings, some boarded up, and vacant lots spread with old litter and junk conveniently half hidden under the blanket of snow. A few cars were parked along the street, mixed with abandoned vehicles without windows or wheels. He couldn't see numbers on the buildings.

In front of one, several men lounged idly, puffing white clouds of breath into the air, looking around, chatting, spitting. Pete got out and went over.

"Is this two-thirty-two?" he said.

The men eyed him from their various perches.

"The only white men come to this neighborhood," drawled one of them, "are cops and basketball coaches."

"I'm not a cop," Pete said.

"Then two-thirty-two's right over there, two doors down. That's where Butch lives."

Suddenly the group loosened into grins for each other and energetically slapped palms with the speaker. "Be careful of Mama," they called as he hurried away.

Pete went through the front door of 232 and knocked on the first door inside. It opened quickly.

"Coach Bell?" the woman said before he could speak. "I'm Lavada McRae. Come right in and have a seat, that one over there."

He went to the worn easy chair she indicated, but he didn't sit down. He stood uncomfortably, trying not to look around at the orderly and clean but tired old apartment. In the kitchen he could see two teenage girls busy with something.

Suddenly he was joined in the room by an old woman who came tottering in with a cane, aided at her elbow by Butch, and she sat silently in an armchair across the room.

"That's my mama," Lavada said, nodding at the expressionless old lady. "And this here's my son, Butch."

Pete shook hands with the handsome boy, who was a couple of inches taller than he was, dressed in neat slacks and sweater. "You played a terrific game yesterday."

"Thank you, sir. Nice of you to say."

He had big hands, long fingers. No surprise, since he had shown he could palm the basketball.

"Sit down, Mr. Bell."

This time Pete obeyed Mrs. McRae's instructions. Butch sat in a straight chair next to him, stretched out his long legs, and clasped his hands together.

"All right, Mr. Bell," the boy's mother said. "I know you're busy, so let's get right down to it. Give me reasons why Butch should travel two thousand miles to go to your school."

"Maybe I should tell you a bit about Western," Pete said, smiling.

"I know about your school. Butch is gonna study science, one kind or another. Tell me about basketball."

"You know we have a terrific science department?"

She met his words with a stony look. "Yes, of course. . . Well, basketball. That's part of Butch's future, which is important."

"And your future?"

"Yes. Right, mine too." This time he acknowledged her with a more honest smile. "The future of all of us." He held out his palms to indicate those in the apartment.

"What are you offering?"

"A full scholarship. Your boy's that good."

"We assume that. That's why you're here. What else?"

"Pardon?"

"Where have you hidden the new car and the extra game tickets to scalp for spending money? There must be some surfer girls."

He couldn't tell how serious she was. He had to assume she was serious. "Mrs. McRae, we don't do that stuff. We don't have to. We have *tradition,* both in the basketball program and in scholarship. Our science department's the best on the West Coast—one of the best in the country."

One of the girls stepped out of the kitchen. "Dinner will be done in eight minutes, Mama."

"Thank you, sweetie," Lavada said, her eyes not leaving Pete.

"Very well-mannered kids," Pete said quietly. "Glad you have St. Joseph's in the area. I'm Catholic, too, by the way."

"I'm not," she said. "I send 'em to Saint Joseph's

because the priests and nuns don't take any sass. *And* they have a good basketball program."

"None taken." He was unsettled. Dawkins had warned him, all right.

"Butch," she said, turning to her son, "is there anything you want to ask Mr. Bell?"

"Well, um . . ." Butch studied his hands. "Los Angeles seems like a long ways away. So I don't know."

"But that's part of education," Pete said, "getting away from home, meeting new people. We'd like you to visit our campus. Would you do that?"

"I don't know. I mean, thank you, I'll think about it. I'm sure it's a nice place."

"It's beautiful, Butch, it really is. I came from Iowa, you know, so it was a long way for me, too. But it's a great place to play, great place to study."

"I'm kind of nervous about college classes, to tell you the truth."

"What about? You're a good student, I understand."

"But college is different."

"The head of the science department is a guy named Dr. George Howe. He's world famous, *and* he's a basketball *nut.*"

"Doctor?"

Pete waggled his hand at Butch. "Don't worry about those titles. He'll make sure you do well."

Lavada stiffened and stuck out her jaw. "Are you implying that the courses are rigged for athletes?"

"No, no, not at all. I just meant that Dr. Howe cares

about his students and will make sure they get all the help they need to learn science. My players take real classes, and my players graduate."

"Well, I heard that. Butch, anything else you want to ask?"

Now Butch looked directly at Pete. "Let me get down to it, coach. If I come to Western, will I be a starter next year?"

Pete hesitated. It was what they all wanted. "You will get the opportunity to start. Let me show you something."

Pete got up and grabbed a floor lamp, and put it in the center of the room, as the McRae family stared at him. "We run a play off the high post cut that you will love—this lamp is our strong side forward—Butch, you're out here at the point." Pete tossed him a pillow. "This is the ball."

One of Butch's sisters stuck her head in the room. "Dinner in two minutes," she announced.

"Sweetheart, c'mere—I want you to guard the lamp."

"The lamp?"

"Now Mrs. McRae, you are the off-guard right here," he said, and reluctantly, Lavada McRae moved into place.

"Grandma, you guard this chair here who is our strong side low post man slid over from the weakside." With some difficulty, Grandma rose from the chair and guarded it as Pete recruited Butch's other sister to guard Butch, which she did with enthusiasm.

"Very simple, Butch, with your quickness you dish it to the off guard—" Pete flipped the pillow to Lavada. "Start right, cut back hard off the lamp, hanging up your sister, you're open for the ball right here—Mom!" Lavada passes the pillow to Butch. "Good!" Pete was in his element.

"Or, Butch you continue down here and pick your sister off the low post for a curl." Pete circled around Grandma, called for the ball, Lavada flipped him the pillow. "And then you explode off this little curl and fill it up all night. I have a whole offense designed to free up a point guard who can shoot."

The room was suddenly silent, the family was stunned. "But will I start?" Butch broke the silence.

"You will probably start."

"Other schools say I *will* start."

Pete capitulated. "You will start."

"Girls, get the dinner on; Butch, get in there and help. Coach Bell and I are going outside to talk."

Pete nervously followed her out into the chilly main corridor near the building's front door.

"You've got a nice family, Mrs. McRae," he said quickly.

"Yes, I do. And I mean to take care of them best I can so long as they need me. Now, Mr. Bell, Butch can't play basketball forever."

"No, ma'am, I—"

"He doesn't understand that yet, but you and I do, so that's okay. He's just a kid. Some decisions he can make, some I make. He will choose the team he wants to play for, and I will choose the science department. We will agree on a college that satisfies both of us."

"I'm sure you will."

"Lot of colleges want my boy."

"I know."

"Everybody says the same thing: great basketball, great school, blah, blah, blah. And I tell 'em all the same thing. My son is not for sale."

"No, no, he shouldn't be. I totally agree."

"But . . ." She paused.

He decided to wait her out. Neither spoke for some seconds, and he didn't let his eyes wander away.

"Mr. Bell," she said finally, "this is a funny world. You need basketball players. My son plays basketball. Several million people a year pay lots of hard-earned money to see a man play basketball. A lot of money to watch tall black men sweat their hearts out to put a ball through a hoop."

"That's true. And we hope these men, black *and* white, have good futures, either in basketball or in other fields. I personally work for that, as a coach and counselor—"

"I am a bus driver," she said, cutting him off. "I don't make diddly. And I hate living in this building in this neighborhood. A bus driver cannot dictate many things in her life, but I do recognize that I'm in a position to dictate a few things at this moment. I can help my family in ways I never could before and never will again."

"Yes."

"Now, my Butch is not going to move far away from me to go to school and play basketball."

"You're ruling out Western?"

"I said not far away from *me*. We are going to get as far away from this neighborhood and this cold as we can get. So where he goes, I plan on moving too, and getting a new and better job."

"Are you saying you would expect us to—"

"I would like a house with a lawn. My children have never had a lawn. Just a raggly old park down there filled with dog doo and junkies."

"Mrs. McRae, I understand and I'm sympathetic. But I have always operated under the NCSA rules. And those rules prohibit giving of gifts, buying of players."

"Mr. Bell, I don't know a great deal about basketball, but I do know this—a foul is not a foul unless the referee blows his whistle. That's *this* part of the basketball game."

Pete began to pace back and forth in the hallway, the cold beginning to stiffen him under his shirt. "I understand the game you're talking about, Mrs. McRae, but let me ask you something. If a young man like Butch starts out at eighteen accepting under-the-table offers, what's he gonna be like in ten years?"

"A millionaire, Mr. Bell. Let me tell you something about values. A boy like Butch, him and the few others you get, they are going to bring millions of dollars in revenues and giving to your university. And help you be rich and famous. Now, I did everything I could do to give him a good home and help him develop. So here he is. You want him. You take him with your other recruits and get millions for your school, and meanwhile I'll still sit here with a lousy job and no lawn. Here's what that says about values. It says, the way you draw it up, *you* get all the values, and there isn't zip left for the people you ride on. Now, Mr. Bell, I'm a good person, and I have a good family, like you said. Somebody out there is gonna make me happy."

She stood there with her arms folded across her ample chest, chin jutting out, eyes wide and firm.

"I'll think about it," Pete said softly.

"You don't have much time," she said, more gently. "Every university in the country wants my son."

"I know. Thank you." She put out her hand and he took it. "I'll have to think about it."

8

SLICK PHIL STOOD IN THE SHADOWS BEHIND THE PRUNED junipers that fronted the Little Belgrade restaurant. There was no particular reason for standing right there except that as a general rule he liked to be out of sight. He did have a reason for standing outside the restaurant rather than waiting inside, because he knew the subtle advantage in walking in with your party, the appearance of being in cahoots.

"Whoa!" spouted Pete, stumbling back at the entrance in surprise at the sudden emergence of the trench coat from the bushes.

"It's me, Pete—Phil. Take it easy."

"Who you hiding from?"

"Who's hiding? I want to talk to you. I've got a hot one."

101

"So you said. Shall we go in? Freddie's probably waiting."

"After you," Phil said, sweeping his arm toward the door.

Freddie was waiting in Pete's usual booth. An iced tea and a large plate of black olives were on the table in front of him. He raised his eyebrows at the sight of Phil approaching behind Pete.

Pete sat down and slid over so Phil could sit next to him. "Hey, Phil," he said quietly, "I got the highest respect for your eye for talent, but there's no such thing these days as a blue-chipper that nobody's ever heard of."

"There was a time nobody'd ever heard of Olajawan, Pippen, Porter," Phil said stiffly.

"Okay, okay," Freddie said, leaning over the olives. "We get the point, Phil."

"Every year I find a blue-chipper everyone else had overlooked, am I right?" Phil looked from one to the other, drawing nods of agreement. "And every decade or so I find somebody that's a franchise, am I right?"

This time Freddie was motionless, and Pete spread his hand and waggled it, indicating so-so.

"Well, look. I think I've found a franchise."

"That nobody knows?"

Phil looked offended.

"Just surprised, that's all."

"Well, I'm not kidding. Have I ever put one over on you? No. This kid, he didn't play high school ball. But I've been watching him for a while because I got a tip from the military." He managed a smug pause. "He played two years in the army in Europe. He grew eight inches and got too big for army regulations. He came home and played a little Jaycee ball in New Mexico. Stopped growing and got his coordination back." He looked back and forth at them. "He showed up at a gym recently and banged with some pros recently, and he kicked butt big-time. Awed those suckers. Then the guy disappeared again."

"And *still* nobody knows?"

"My phone's ringing off the hook because everyone knows I'm on to *somebody*. Nobody's got the name. Nobody knows where he is. Except me."

Freddie exhaled through pursed lips and shook his head.

"Why are you bringing this to me instead of other coaches? Since when are you such a fan?"

"'Cause even though this kid's a project with a lot of rough edges, your program's so screwed up right now. I know my boy'll move right into the starting lineup." Phil sat back in the booth and puffed out his chest.

"You're making a lot of assumptions," Pete said.

"You think I'm exaggerating?" Phil looked back and forth. "Want to hop a plane and meet my kid? You think I don't know where he is? He's in Algiers." He was met with shocked looks. "Louisiana, guys. Come on, what do you think I am? Algiers, Louisiana, little old backwater section across the river from New Orleans."

* * *

The shrimp boat stank, of both fish and fuel, and the early morning fog over the river seemed to close them in with the stink. New Orleans disappeared quickly astern. When they reached the small boat landing, they could have been anywhere, Pete thought. They climbed off the chugging shrimper and walked inland, past a faded wooden sign that said ALGIERS. The low buildings were ramshackle, run-down, with elements of what Pete presumed could be French or even Moorish influence.

"This could be Algiers, Algeria, for all I know. Where are we headed, Phil?"

Phil pointed ahead, and from the fog emerged an awning and then the front of a bar that had just half a sign left over the front: TUT.

They went in.

"Nothing quite like an old bar first thing in the morning," Pete said, wrinkling his nose at the rancid odor. "But I guess it's better than the stinkin' boat."

When their eyes adjusted to the dim light, Phil led him past a table where a card game was in progress, to the bar.

"Wait here," Phil said, in his mysterious, conspiratorial way. "I gotta see the man."

He went to the rear of the room, where a large black man was seated on a tall stool with a phone to his ear and a racing form in his hand. They had a few whispered words, the big man nodded, and Phil waved for Pete to join them.

"Pete, Antoine," Phil said out of the corner of his mouth.

Pete nodded. Antoine grunted.

"Let's go," Antoine said.

They went out the back door, through an alley, across a thickly overgrown lot, into a neighborhood of scurrying barefoot black children, old black people sitting on the leaning porches of small old faded wood houses, mangy sniffing dogs, and suspicious young black men eyeing them silently as they passed.

Then they were out of that small residential neighborhood and slogging through some fields tall with vines and briers and heavy with humidity. They came eventually upon a big warehouse looming out of the fog like a Hollywood soundstage.

They entered through a small side door and found themselves amid a clutter of huge, colorful, tattered remnants of what could have been stage sets.

"Old Mardi Gras floats," Antoine said. "Take care y'all don't catch your leg in none a that."

mThey climbed through the debris and stopped. The rear half of the building contained a basketball court, and a game was in progress. Three on three, with other groups sitting on the floor along the sides, evidently waiting their turn to play.

Dominating the game was a huge man who whirled toward the hoop and leaped clear of the others, majestic as Everest among the lesser peaks, and slammed the ball through the basket with a whoomp that resounded through the huge hollow steel edifice.

"All yours," Antoine said, holding his palm out to Phil.

Phil slapped some bills into the palm. "Be in touch."

Antoine didn't respond, just turned and was gone.

"So what do you think?" Phil asked.

"One dunk in a street game doesn't mean anything."

"I mean the *size*, the *strength*."

"He's big."

The man took a pass, head-faked, took two quick dribbles, and then soared again and drove the ball down through the basket, leaving the structure quivering.

"He's a monster, Pete, a monster. You never saw anything like this guy, am I right?"

"I've seen Chamberlain."

"Yeah, but I mean, a *kid*, a *youth*, a *beginner*."

"Does he have a name?"

"Neon Bodeaux." Phil spelled it.

"Neon Bodeaux. Neon? What's his real name?"

"That's it—Neon. French. It means—"

"It means neon."

"Probably. Pete, he's never even really been coached. Think of the raw material. What a natural, with the right training. That's why I want him with you. Seven-one, 295 pounds, quick feet—well, I don't have to sell this kid, you can see for yourself."

"Speaking of selling," Pete said, as the players thundered down the court, "what's in this for you?"

"Me? Don't worry about it." Phil gave a dismissive wave.

An opponent went up for a jumper, and Neon

soared out of nowhere, emitting a deep grunt, to slam the ball backwards where it rocketed beyond the court and bonged into the steel wall.

"Little hard to judge him here," Pete said.

"Oh, come on, Pete!" Phil spun away, then turned back. "Don't tell me you can't see the talent. I told you he's a project. But he's a *monster.*"

Neon glided through the air to sink a bank shot from ten feet.

"You know anything about his head?" Pete asked.

Phil sighed. "He ain't Einstein, okay? Whadaya want?"

"How much of an Einstein is he not?"

"I had him take a Scholastic Aptitude Test recently, okay? Just like a high school kid. He scored five-twenty."

"He got five twenty out of sixteen hundred? You get four hundred just for spelling your name right."

Phil shrugged. "Tough name. Hey, Neon! Big guy, over here!" He motioned their way.

Neon flipped the ball in the air and ambled over. "'Sup, Phil?"

"Neon, my man, meet Coach Petey Bell of the Western University Dolphins!"

Neon's hand was as big as a ham, and it dwarfed Pete's as they shook.

"All the way out here?" Neon said, eyeing Pete up and down.

"Let's take a walk," Phil said.

Either the pavement was muddy or the street was just mud—Pete couldn't tell as he walked beside

Neon through the residential neighborhood they had passed earlier. Phil dropped a few discreet steps behind.

"So, Neon, you ever think about going to college?"

"Thought about it a couple times. I could get into that, play some hoops, hang out. Don't know about them courses."

"We can help you there. There's a thing called Proposition Forty-eight, which says that if your grades aren't up to par you can still get into college if you get seven hundred on your S.A.T. scores. That's to help guys like you who are smart but haven't done so well in school."

"Them tests are culturally biased."

Pete glanced up at him to see if there was an ironic smile. There was no smile. "Well, the whole world's culturally biased, Neon. What else is new? We're just talking about getting into college."

"Huh." Neon waved to somebody he knew. "All the way here for that. Would you be trying to help me get into college if I couldn't play basketball?"

"No."

Neon chuckled, a deep, husky rumble. "Well, least you're honest."

Phil came skipping up. "I told you, Pete's the straightest shooter in—"

"Shut up, Phil," Pete said evenly.

"You got it, Coach." Phil saluted and dropped back again.

"You mind me trying to help you, Neon?" Pete asked.

"I pretty much mind myself, Mr. Bell. But, to be fair, no, I don't mind, so long as you play straight."

"Would you be willing to work with a tutor?"

"You mean studying and stuff?"

"Yup. Part of the package."

"No problem."

"Good. Good start."

After they'd walked in silence for a while, they began to hear music. They approached a small, sagging church, once white, whose front doors were propped open. They stopped and looked in. A heavy drumbeat accompanied the driving chords of an organ, and the congregation was swaying and clapping and belting out a hymn.

"What kinda church is this?" Pete asked, beginning to sway to the music.

"Assemblies of God."

"A Pentecostal church? Aw, man, I grew up in the Pentecostal church!"

"Do tell," Neon said with an ironic smile, watching Pete close his eyes and snap his fingers and sway.

Slick Phil stood off behind a thick rhododendron, watching nervously the developments in which he had a considerable stake.

9

JENNY USHERED OUT HER FIRST GRADE CLASS AT THE END of the day. "The songs were wonderful, kids. I'll see you tomorrow. Don't forget your shamrocks."

She returned to her desk and began putting things away. A shadow fell over her, and she looked up. "Pete!"

"This is Neon Bodeaux," Pete said, clapping Neon on the back.

Her mouth dropped open, and she looked back and forth from one to the other.

"Hello, ma'am," Neon said, shifting uncomfortably from one foot to the other.

"What's going on?"

"Neon's going to need some tutoring."

"I'm sorry, Neon," Jenny said, shaking her head and sighing, "that was rude. Forgive me." She stuck out her hand. "Nice to meet you. Okay, now . . ." She turned to Pete.

"I can explain."

She waited.

Pete said, "Um."

She waited.

"Neon needs some tutoring."

"You said that." She cocked her head and narrowed her eyes. "Don't even think about it."

"What's that, Jen?"

"Me. You're here to ask me to tutor him. I haven't tutored college students in years. Not since Tony. Neon, I'm sorry. This doesn't concern you. Well, yes it does, but . . ."

A child scampered in and grabbed a pencil off the table.

"Don't step on any children, Neon!"

"I'll try not to."

"I feel totally addled."

"You look fine, Jen."

"Stop it! Just stop it! Now, look." She held her hands out, palms down. "You come cruising in here at the end of the day when I'm all frazzled, and spring this on me."

"It's important. Jenny is the best tutor in the conference, Neon. Jen, remember the 'eighty-four team? You helped get the whole front line into school."

111

"Yeah, and I helped keep them in school for four years. That was then. This is now."

"Let's have a cup of coffee. Neon, would you excuse us?"

"Wait a minute." Jenny waved her hands.

"Certainly, Coach. Hope to see you again, ma'am." Neon walked out, an impossible giant in these elementary school halls. Children pressed against the walls and stopped to gawk at him.

"Wait a minute," Jenny hissed.

"Come on, we'll go over to the Belgrade."

They sat with cups of coffee, and Pete recounted the tale of Neon Bodeaux.

"Jiminy," Jenny said. "Kind of unbelievable."

"I know."

"What happened to Butch McRae and Ricky Roe?"

"I'm working on them."

"So now this Neon Bodeaux is a 'project,' as you say, like Tony was. Tony was a known player, though."

"So what? The point is, you helped Tony get in, and look how good he's doing now."

"You said he was flunking TV."

"It's a tough course. They don't just sit and watch the tube, you know." He turned the cup in his hands and stared at it. "Just what was so tough about living with me?"

"Let's see . . ." Jenny sighed and clucked. "You were all basketball, you were moody, depending on how that was going, and we just had a different kind of rhythm about life. I wasn't having a good time, that's all."

"Rhythm?"

"Ups, downs, interests, like that."

"You love basketball."

"Pete, don't try to pick it all apart. There's no exact specifics. Give it a rest. We're here because you wanted to tell me about Neon Bodeaux. Are you finished?"

"Poor kid doesn't have a father. For all I know, he doesn't even have a mother."

"Why do you think that?"

"He never says anything about having a mother."

"Oh, Pete, can it. Can he rebound?"

"He's a monster, totally dominant inside, both ends."

"What's his S.A.T. score?"

"Five hundred and twenty big ones."

"Ouch!"

"The tests are culturally biased."

"Now you're a sociologist?"

"He is very bright. He should be a good student. He just needs a jump start."

"Yeah, sure. So he can dominate the basketball court for you."

"Well, why else would I have him here? Anyway, it's not just for me."

"No, you're right. That wasn't fair." She took a deep breath. "Just for you, no, I wouldn't do it. For Neon, maybe. For Tony, yes, okay. The combination.

It would be nice to see Tony have a little help in his senior year."

"Terrific! Great! Thank you! You're wonderful!" He pushed himself up and leaned across the table to kiss her.

"Don't kiss me. This one's for the ball club," she said, quickly leaning away.

"But you called—"

"That was then."

Pete sat in the Hot Seat, flanked by the pep band, Dolph the mascot and the cheerleaders, and fielded in a sort of blank state the typical unanswerable postseason questions: Why did you have a bad season? How will you have a good one? Because we didn't play well, I didn't coach well. By playing better, coaching better, having better players.

Then Ed Axelby shuffled to the mike. Pete steeled himself to maintain his casually gruff demeanor.

"Ed, this show is for fans, not sportswriters. You get to unload on me every day in that rag of yours."

"You've been ducking my calls lately," Ed retorted.

"Yeah, I don't talk to arsonists or child molesters, either." Pete spit out his reply, and the crowd oohed.

"Coach Bell, I have received strong indications from reliable sources that unless you have a great recruiting season you are likely to be replaced as head coach. You care to give me a quote on that?"

"Yeah," Pete responded, glaring at the reported. "'You can lead a horse to water, but unless you can teach him to float on his back, you ain't got diddly-squat.' Quote that."

After the chuckles died down, Axelby said, "Are you affirming or denying the rumor?"

"I'm giving you a quote. Who's next?"

A rustle of whispers spread through the audience, and another questioner started for the mike, but Axelby held on—this time with an even more aggressive tone.

"One more question, sir. Is it true that you have become so desperate that you are trying to recruit a semiliterate twenty-year-old who did not even play high school basketball?"

Pete ground his teeth and dug his fingers into his thighs. "Whose garbage are you playing in, Ed?" He turned to the crowd. "You know what happens to a guy who fails at sports and then fails at writing. He becomes a sportswriter."

Pete stood up quicker than he meant to, knocking over the Hot Seat—a clumsiness that further frustrated him—and made a fist from which he pointed an index finger at Axelby. "I'm tired of talking to you inside, Axelby. Let's go outside to the parking lot and get to the heart of the matter, huh?"

He took a couple of steps toward Axelby. People started to scatter. TV people started talking into their headset mikes. The band director waved his hands to get the band ready to play.

"You're crazy, Bell!" Axelby hollered.

"You know the difference between being crazy and

being colorful?" Pete bellowed back, jumping down off the stage. "Winning—that's the difference. C'mon, Ed, I'll kick your butt."

Pete swatted aside the microphone stand, but Axelby had already turned and ducked into the crowd, several of whom were now pushing forward to interrupt Pete's charge. People grabbed his arms and held his shoulders.

"I'm okay, I'm okay," Pete said, nodding this way and that to reassure his handlers. They let him go. He shrugged his jacket back into place on his shoulders and stomped out the side exit.

There might be a price to pay, Pete thought as he sat down on the barstool at the Little Belgrade. They would edit out the worst of it. But word would get around that he'd popped his gizzard, and Axelbrains would have fun with him in print. There was no defense for something like this. Axelby was widely regarded as a humorless maggot, even among the press. But what could you say? The guy wasn't a child molester.

And the truth of it was, the problem was losing. Losing was bad enough without losing it in front of everybody. Well, no going back. He'd just josh it through.

The young bartender swabbed a spot in front of Pete. "So, Coach, what'll it be?"

"The usual."

"What's that?"

"I'll have what my friend here is having."

"Coach, you're the only one here."

"It's a *joke,* Smitty! Lighten up, and give me the usual. Make it a double."

Smitty put two nonalcholic beers on the bar. "Sounds like you're having a rough day."

"Aw, lost my cookies at that dufus Axelby, taping my show. And just trying to pull it together after the season. Starting to feel the pressure, I guess."

"Sure was simpler when I played for you, Coach."

"Things weren't so frantic. How many games did we lose in your four years at Western?"

"Six my freshman year, then five, then two. Then the year we won it all, we lost that one game to Indiana."

"That's fourteen in four years, Smitty. We lost fifteen this year. *Fifteen.* Can you imagine? Tell me straight, Smitty. You know the game. Be honest. Am I losing it?"

"You're asking a bartender to be honest?"

"Come on."

"You know you're not losing it, Coach. You just don't have the horses. I don't know why you don't."

"Yes, you do."

"I have my theories. I liked it your way. Uh-oh, the slime is here." Smitty nodded discreetly toward a booth.

Pete waited a few seconds, then turned casually to see the fat, florid face of Happy Kuykendall atop his sloppy shoulders grinning out of the booth. Pete winced and turned back. Not quick enough.

"Petey!" Happy's call was a buzz saw hitting bad

117

wood. "Hey, great job, Petey, beatin' up that sports-writer. He's a jerk. They're all a bunch a jerks."

"I didn't beat up anybody, you bozo," Pete growled into his beer mug, trying to appear to ignore him.

"Hey, Petey, turn around. Come on over."

Pete didn't turn.

"Hey, Petey, why you hate me so much?"

Now he turned. "Because you and the fifty thousand alumni you represent are obnoxious, spoiled slobs, immoral and unethical pea-brains."

"Hey"—Happy spread his arms—"that's not all bad, right?" He firmed up his mouth and narrowed his eyes. "What you oughta be grateful for is that, unlike most of them, I remain firmly in your ever-shrinking corner."

"You ain't worth rat dip."

"Hey, great. Glad to see you can still get your hackles up at your age. You were a better coach when you could get mad and stay mad."

"Oh, get lost. I'm outta here. Smitty, you oughta fumigate this place. 'Night."

He scooted out. Not quick enough. He was entering the parking lot when he heard Happy behind him.

"Hey, Coach, why you walking away from me? Come on, wait up. You have never walked away from anything in your life."

Happy trotted up behind him. "I *know* you, buster!"

"You don't know squat-diddly bupkis."

"Au contraire. I know everything." Happy fell in alongside him. He smelled of Boca Raton. "I know

what Butch McRae's mother wants. I know what Ricky Roe is gonna want. I know you've got a kid named Neon Bodeaux being tutored by your ex-wife."

Pete stopped like a lassoed calf and turned to face his smug tormentor. "Huh?"

"And I know that the amount of money it will take to buy out your contract is roughly the same as the amount of money it will take to ensure that Butch and Ricky sign letters of intent to play basketball at Western University."

Happy had his chin stuck out in a most inviting position, but Pete resisted. "Western University doesn't buy athletes."

"Who said anything about buy? You've been alone too long, Petey boy. We're talking about recruiting, a most urbane art involving the most imaginative artisans."

"Western's programs are clean."

"Petey, Petey, please. You should know, if you don't already, that our football team has been ranked in the top ten for eight straight years, correct? We have on the current roster a linebacker, tailback, offensive tackle, two safeties, and a quarterback who were recruited right out of this box."

"I don't like football."

"All those boys are graduating this year. Graduating! You see, there's a difference between clean and washed. My money is untraceable—washed scrubbed and laundered within an inch of its life. Ollie North woulda never gone to trial if he'd known me."

"Then you got a future in politics, jerk—you

oughta run for office." Pete turned to go. Happy stopped him again, this time with a hand on his shoulder.

"Hey, hey, Coach. Get off your high horse for one minute of your life. These athletes generate millions for the university. Am I wrong or right? What do the kids get? Nothing. And by the way, what do you get?"

"What?"

"You got a multi-year contract. You get six figures for a shoe contract so that your team can be a walking billboard and that's all legal. You get six figures for your TV show so you can beat up on people. All absolutely legal. You can dust off your hands and be cleaner than God. You're doing okay, Pete. Am I right or wrong?"

Pete grabbed Happy's lapels in his fists, enjoying for the briefest instant the terror in Happy's rheumy eyes before realizing that there were other eyes in the parking lot, turned toward them, and he could ill afford a second public episode in the same day. He released Happy's jacket and smoothed the front solicitously, saying in a low and ordinary voice: "Stay outta my face and don't ever speak to me again."

As Pete walked away, he heard the hoarse whisper: "We *owe* them this money!"

10

NEON HUNCHED OVER JENNY'S KITCHEN TABLE, FORE-
head propped on his fingers, staring at a map of the
Western Hemisphere with no names on it. Jenny sat at
the other side of the table tapping her foot.

"All right," she said, maintaining a strenuous patience, "let's make it easier. What is the country
located immediately north of the United States?"

"Spain?"

"Wrong. What is the country located immediately
south of the United States?"

"Canada."

"You're full of it, and you know it. I'll give you fifty
dollars if you can tell me the country located immediately to the south of the United States."

"Mexico." He planted his oak finger smack in the

121

middle of the outline of Mexico, then moved it along the map, jabbing each country as he spoke. "Then Guatemala, Belize, Honduras, Nicaragua, El Salvador, Costa Rica, Panama. That'll be fifty dollars."

"You were lying, playing dumb. I was lying about the fifty."

"You gotta be nuts."

"Yeah, I was married to Pete. What's your excuse?"

"I'm not nuts."

"You're not dumb, either. So why the act?"

Neon leaned back and crossed his arms. "You start off insulting me with third grade geography questions."

"I didn't know anything about you. How could I know what level you were at?"

"Where I'm at is I'm a man, not just a shufflin', shiftless boy. But you assume I'm ignorant. Beneath your politically correct facade, you're a racist too."

"Too?"

"I mean, like everybody else around here."

"Maybe I'm ignorant and *you're* the racist."

"Er-uh . . ."

"Let's just cut the crap, okay? We're both smart. The idea is to get you in here to play basketball. That's not for my sake. If you don't want to, fine, I've got plenty to do. But I'd like to help. Up to you."

Neon shrugged.

"Why'd you score five-twenty on your S.A.T.s?"

"Felt like it."

"Terrific. What sense am I supposed to make out of that?"

Neon rubbed his chin. "The neighborhood I grew up in was so dangerous that I joined the army and invaded the Persian Gulf for a vacation. I was too big to fit inside anything, so I was willing to just walk on into Baghdad on my own and slam-dunk Saddam, if that'd make everybody happy. But it didn't work out anyway. So I came home and looked for hoops to fill. I don't ask anybody for anything. I make my own sense. I don't know who's gonna make yours."

"I see." She wearily pushed herself up and went to the counter. "Coffee?"

"Okay."

She set a cup in front of him and sat down, leaned on her elbows, and rested her chin on her clasped hands. "So why are we here?"

"I'm here because maybe I want to go to college and maybe I don't. I won't know until I get in and find out if college is as phony as everything else."

"Excuse me, but I'm not here just to be part of all the phony stuff. I got a hundred dollars says you can't get seven hundred on your S.A.T.s."

"Save your money. You see, that too is an insult disguising itself as a motivational speech."

"What's the insult?"

"Thinking you just waggle your dollars."

"All I know is, my splendid motivational words don't do anything. The only thing that's worked with you so far is to offer you fifty bucks."

"That was a lie."

Jenny smiled slyly. "So, what's this? I bet a hundred. You believe me this time?"

"I could score seven hundred in my sleep. For a hundred dollars I'll score eight hundred."

"Oh, really?"

"Proper."

Pete strode through the door, causing them both to jump. "What's going on? Doesn't anybody answer the doorbell anymore?"

"We were haggling," Jenny said.

"Your old lady's tough," Neon said.

"My *ex*-old lady's tough." Pete pulled out a chair, turned it around, and straddled it backwards. "How's it going, ex?"

"He doesn't need tutoring," Jenny said, staring at Neon. "He needs a kick in the pants."

"Well, Neon," Pete said, "what's your opinion of what you need?"

"I need a paycheck."

"Sometimes a kick in the pants and a paycheck are the same thing," Pete told him.

"You'll be making millions," Jenny grumbled, "while I'll still be cutting out valentines with first graders."

"I ain't tutoring you."

"There's a test in two weeks," Jenny said to Pete. "He should sign up to take it."

"And get the hundred ready," Neon said, smiling broadly as he rose from his chair. "Eight hundred's a lock."

He ambled out, hands jammed in his pockets, whistling tunelessly.

They watched him go, then stood looking around the kitchen uncomfortably.

"Sorry I just walked in like that," Pete said. "You know I never would—"

"It's okay."

"So, uh, you doing anything later? I mean, want to go out for a cup of coffee or something?"

"I'm free . . ." She paused, then suddenly made a quick correction. "Actually I've got, uh, something."

"Something?"

"Something."

Pete nodded, somehow relieved.

"So good luck in Indiana."

"How'd you know I was going to Indiana?"

"I'm psychic. You've been to Chicago. Ricky Roe's in Indiana."

"You're going out?"

"What? *Now?*"

"You said . . ."

"I've got something to do. That what you mean? Here. I'm not going anywhere. Pete." She put a hand on his arm. "Don't make it difficult every time."

"Okay. I better get home."

"Good luck in Indiana," she repeated.

11

BUT YOU HAVE TO *YIELD* TO HIM, OPEN UP YOURSELF and let *Him* come in, and then can you have the peace you so desperately crave. . . ."

The spring snows were gone. The rolling farmlands were moist and black, with the first hints of green stippling the fields, making them look furry in the distance.

Pete guided his rented Taurus off the interstate and onto a two-lane state highway that led off among the cornfields. From time to time he checked the Indiana map spread open on the seat beside him.

"Oh, *yes*, let Jesus come into your heart. . . ."

The local evangelist on the radio took Pete back to his childhood—the part he'd hated. He had hated going to church. When he was little, the ranting had scared him. When he was a little older, it had bored him. Now he didn't mind it. It was a familiar type of voice and message. Indiana wasn't Iowa, but still it made him feel a little bit like he was home.

He turned off this highway onto a smaller road and drove through a small town, a village, then turned again and again. Surrounded by fields, he saw a farmer at a mailbox and stopped to ask directions. The farmer pointed straight ahead.

Pete drove over a rise and past several smaller farms until he saw the gate to an estate—an unlikely vision in these environs. He turned in. The broad, rolling grounds unfolded as he drove along. Abruptly, beyond a grove of trees, he came upon an outdoor basketball court. At the far end were two men in street clothes watching a third, also in street clothes, shoot jumpers.

Pete parked and walked over. "White farm boy with a basketball? You'll never make it, son."

The shooter, just getting ready to hoist another shot, broke into a laugh. "That's what I heard," Larry Bird said. "Can't jump, can't run. How's it going, Pete?"

"I'm okay. How's your back?"

"Pathetic." The retired star of the Boston Celtics shook his head. "Now I *really* can't run and jump."

"Your shot still looks good."

"Long as I don't have to do it night after night. What brings you out here?" His blond hair was short and sparse. He led Pete over to some chairs, and they sat down.

"Just happened to be in the neighborhood."

"Yeah, you and every other coach in the country—and I know you ain't here to see me."

"Larry, Larry, we're pals." Pete chuckled, too. "How about all those years I spoke at your basketball camp for free? All those stock tips I gave you, for free? Haven't I—"

"Cut the bull, Pete, Nothing's free? Isn't that what you always used to tell me? Whatta ya want?"

"You know the kid."

"There's a parade tomorrow to honor the team. Want to come along?"

"Has Busher been around?"

"Yup."

"Okay. Get me into the parade."

"You got it, Coach."

Heading the parade down the center of the town of French Lick was a banner: Indiana State High School Champs, The French Lick Red Devils. Then came baton twirlers and marching bands separated by tractors, pickups, and backhoes draped with red and white streamers.

In the midst of all this, surrounded by the twirlers and bands and tractors and celebrants, were two Mercury convertibles carrying the teenage boys who were the Red Devils.

People pressed along the curbs waving pennants

and balloons; small children perched on the shoulders of adults.

"Here they are!" the announcer's voice came over the hand-held megaphone from a small reviewing stand in the middle of the block. "The champs themselves! Show 'em how proud we are!"

People yelled and hollered and waved; twirlers spun their batons; the bands played marches. The convertibles edged through the street toward the main part of the crowd of spectators.

"And now a very special treat!" the announcer crowed. "Riding with our own All-State star, Ricky Roe, is a last-minute honorary grand Marshal. I give you the man who went from the Red Devils red and white to the clover green of the great Boston Celtics . . . the one and only, our very own, Larry Bird!"

He paused to allow the cheers to swell and subside. "And they are in a vehicle driven by Coach Pete Bell of Western University, who's won two national championships—Pete Bell!"

Larry Bird and Ricky Roe sat on top of the backseat, waving their clasped hands in the air. Pete waved and scanned the crowd. At last he saw what he was looking for and managed a wide grin and a thumbs-up.

Busher and other coaches here to recruit Ricky Roe looked on stoically. Only Busher returned the wave.

That evening Pete joined Ricky and his family in their comfortable old farmhouse.

"Welcome to Indiana, Mr. Bell," said Ricky's father, a sturdy blond man, holding out a meaty, callused hand from which was missing the last segment of the forefinger.

"Call me Pete."

"I'd rather keep it businesslike, if you don't mind."

"Sure, fine, Mr. Roe." The farmer's tone was not unfriendly, just careful.

"So, Ricky," Pete turned to the tall, broad-shouldered, crew-cut seventeen-year-old, "what direction do you see your college studies taking you?"

"I don't know. I hadn't really, you know, decided."

"Well, there's no reason to decide right away."

"He'd like to take over the farm someday down the road," his father said.

"I would?"

"Sure. What else could anybody want? The natural thing. Carry on the business. Right, Mr. Bell?"

"I guess it depends on a lot of things," Pete said. "Can be a nice life, on a farm, if that's what you like."

"Who wouldn't?"

"The truth is," Ricky said, "I haven't even made up my mind if I want to go to college."

His mother, a heavy, sweet-faced woman, had just come down the stairs to join them. "Now, Ricky," she said in a voice like waggling a finger, "you know you have, so don't talk like that. Mr. Bell came a long way to visit you."

"Maybe I shouldn't be here," Pete said, suddenly uncomfortable.

"No, no, Coach," Ricky said, smiling shyly, "I'm

glad you came. I'm just sometimes, well, immature. I guess that's what you call it. I guess I'm just sort of uncertain about some things."

"You're way ahead of me at your age," Pete said, "because I was truly immature and didn't know it. Honesty is the first step toward maturity."

"That's what we tell him," his mother said, smiling and nodding.

"What I really want to do is shoot some hoops," Ricky said. "Want to go outside?"

"Sure."

"Okay, Ma?"

"Of course, dear."

"Show him how you can shoot the eyes out of the basket," his father said.

There was a hoop mounted over the barn door. Ricky leaned a plywood sheet against the door.

"I gotta ask you, Ricky," Pete said, "you're not sure about college, you don't know if you want to work your father's farm. What *are* you interested in?"

"Girls." Ricky hoisted a soft shot that swished through. The ball bounced off the angled plywood and returned to him. He shot again. "Girls and hoops."

"Nothing wrong with that. Far as it goes. We got millions of girls at Western. And of course you know about our hoops."

"Yeah, I do." Ricky shot again and again, each time the ball bouncing right back to him. His delivery was flawless. The kid could easily take on another twenty pounds of muscle.

"But you have an opportunity now to get an education using your basketball skills," Pete said. "That's your good luck. You know what a lot of kids would give to be in your shoes. Whether you come to Western or not, you should get an education. Girls will always be around, the rest of your life."

"It ain't so simple." Ricky dribbled behind his back and between his legs, then hit a quick jumper. "See, around here we're all a bunch of Baptists. I mean, if you go out on a date, your folks think you should marry the girl."

"Oh, yeah? Your folks are like that?"

"Pretty much."

"Maybe it's time to get away from your parents."

"Yeah, probably," Ricky said wistfully. "But you still gotta deal with my father."

"Well, sure, we all should discuss things and agree."

"It ain't so simple."

The ball whanged off the plywood and hopped back to Pete. He fielded it and threw up a shot that hit the barn.

"I brought some coffee," called Mr. Roe, striding out from the house with two cups. "Let's go over there and set down."

They went to the side of the barn and sat on two stumps near an old red Farmall tractor with a rusty four-row disk plow attached.

"My boy can shoot," Mr. Roe said, watching his son.

"That he can. He sure can."

"He can do the rest of it, too."

"I imagine he can."

"I mean defense, rebound, the whole deal."

"He has a terrific reputation. I'm sure you're right. But I guess the question is, does he want to go to college?"

"I might have some influence over that."

"You should have."

"Lot of coaches have been by here."

"You should be proud. . . ."

"Funny thing. They asked me what I needed."

"You mean to be convinced—"

"And I told 'em I needed a new tractor. Oh, I got another one inside, an old International diesel. But it's a struggle to make it on a small farm anymore. You gotta make every day count, every minute. You can't have old equipment breakin' down on you every time you flip the hydraulics or engage the power takeoff. Farmers these days, they gotta have four-wheel drive, or at least dual rears. Gotta have a closed cab 'cause of the dust that kills you over the years. And air conditioning 'cause a closed cab will bake you alive in the sun otherwise. That's why farmers die young, 'cause they take such a beating. So to compete nowadays you got to have modern equipment—nothing too fancy, just stuff that runs every day and pulls its load and keeps you from having a heart attack."

They were silent for a moment, the only sound being the ball bouncing, swishing through the net, ricocheting off the plywood.

"A tractor," Pete said.

"What's that?" Mr. Roe cupped a hand behind his ear as if he hadn't heard.

"You asked for a tractor."

"Oh, I didn't mean to ask for nothing. I just was saying that I keep getting asked what I need by this school and that. I don't know nothing about rules. I mean, whatever your rules are don't make me no never mind. Whatever they are, they ain't my rules. My rules are just you work your head off every single day."

"But you're suggesting that someone's going to give you a tractor. Some school."

"That's what I'm saying." He nodded thoughtfully. "But I know I want my boy to go with a coach that's gonna watch over him."

"How's that?"

"I'd like him to be with a . . . well, a churchgoing type."

"For what it's worth, Mr. Roe, I was raised in the Baptist church. I was taught to respect the fundamentals, and you never forget those lessons, not if you believed the way I have."

Mr. Roe turned to him and peered through narrowed eyes. "First Baptist or Southern Baptist?"

Pete nodded as he quickly calculated the odds. "First Baptist, of course."

"Good man." Mr. Roe stood up and stretched, then came over and put a hand on Pete's shoulder. "I thank the good Lord for you, Mr. Bell. We don't think much of Southern Baptists around here."

"I'm relieved to hear that."

"We'll be in touch, then?"

"I'm sure we will, Mr. Roe. I hope the idea of Western appeals to you. He would love our basketball program."

"Well, Mr. Bell, I'm mostly just a regular farmer, you see. Just trying to scratch out a living right here."

"I understand."

12

PETE LUGGED HIS SUITCASE INTO HIS OFFICE, TO WHICH he had come direct from the plane, and plopped down on the sofa with a sigh. These excursions weren't as much fun as they used to be, when the thrill of the chase was newer and the kids weren't so blasé about the chance to play big-time college sports.

Mel walked in. "Hey, Pete. How'd it go?"

"Lotta corn in Indiana. But I think I got a visit outta Ricky."

"That's great. Larry was helpful?"

"He comes on like such a hayseed that people are always surprised how slick he is. Yeah, he slipped me in at the head of the line."

"Then we may have hit the daily double, because Lavada McRae called last night. She said Butch will visit on one condition: that he meets with Dr. Howe and gets a tour of the science department."

"That's all?"

"That's all she said. But I'm sure the rest of the stuff is still on the table—the job, the house and lawn."

Pete sighed and laid his head back and closed his eyes. "What's the matter with people?"

"People just pick the routes set out for them, that's all. We didn't make the rules, good *or* bad. Neither did they."

"Yeah, but we've always *followed* the rules. Whatever happened to law-abiding citizens?"

"There's rules and there's rules." Mel chuckled. "You know what they say: Show me a law-abiding citizen, I'll show you an honest politician."

There was a knock at the door, and Jenny poked her head in. "Hi, guys. Can I come in?"

"What's up?" Pete popped up from the sofa.

"I've got a surprise for you. Mr. Bodeaux?" She ushered Neon in. He ducked through the door, holding a sheet of paper.

"Nine hundred and sixty," Neon announced, fluttering the paper at them.

"He improved by four hundred forty points on his S.A.T.s!" Jenny sang.

"Somebody owes me a hundred U.S. dollars," Neon said.

"Wow! Sensational!" Pete grabbed his arm and shook Neon's mighty hand. "How'd you do that?"

"Your ex called me out, that's all. Had to get down to it."

"He could score whatever he wanted to," Jenny said.

"I wouldn't have believed it."

"Imagine that," Mel said. "Something that big got a brain way up on top of it after all."

Neon guffawed and stepped over to slap Mel's upraised palm. It sounded like a gunshot.

"Mel, take Mr. Bodeaux to the admissions office and introduce him around," Pete said, patting Neon's back. "Tell 'em we got ourselves a potential Rhodes Scholar, but we're gonna try to talk him into playing basketball, too."

He watched them leave. "That's some job, Jenny. Thanks."

"Don't mention it. Anyway, he didn't need any tutoring."

"Buy you a coffee, over at the Market?"

"Hey, big spender, don't mind if I do."

The soft southern California dusk was spreading over the Grand Central Market when they took a café table. He fought the grim tide of nostalgia that so often threatened to flood him when he sat with Jenny at his favorite time of day, in the seductive clutch of this tropical, if smoggy, air.

"I really appreciate your help," he said, leaning a little over the table and hoping she'd reach for his hand.

But she didn't. She leaned back sideways in her chair and crossed her legs and teased her brown hair. "Anything for a power forward, eh?"

"Yeah, yeah, but the other two guys, the two legitimate blue-chippers, McRae and Roe, I'd have to break the rules to get them. They want money, jobs, crazy stuff—you know what I'm talking about."

"Sure. It's in the papers all the time. Programs called on the carpet for violations."

He chuckled sardonically. "Those old farts over at the NCSA. Keystone Kops. They're just watching out for themselves. They don't care about the game or the quality of the values we teach the kids or anything. They police as little as possible."

"Speaking of the papers, as I was, any fallout from that dustup with Ed Axelby at your show?"

"Jokes, snickers, that's all."

"Don't be too hard on him. He's just a guy."

"Hard is not hard enough. He's a mean, small-minded maggot."

"I think he's lonely."

"Oh, man."

"Just like a woman, huh?"

Pete clenched his teeth and felt tripped up and stupid.

"Are you thinking of cheating, Pete?"

The intimacy of the question gave him a twinge. She was so cool and controlled. "The rules that govern college athletics are hypocritical crap."

"Bravo."

"Well, I mean it."

"Look, Pete, I'm not your mother and I'm not your wife and I'm not your priest . . . although at one time I think I was all three."

"You were," Pete said affectionately. She leaned over and covered his hand with hers. "I know that you were never unfaithful during our marriage—I absolutely know it. I know that you never get a parking ticket you don't pay, you never walk when it says 'don't walk,' and the one time you lied to me about a surprise birthday party, you were a dead giveaway. You don't even know how to lie about a birthday party! You don't lie. You don't cheat. Oh, I know about your wily little fibs to boys and their parents when you're on a recruiting trip or something. But on anything important, you are the straightest guy I have ever known. You are also brilliant at your profession. You're tying yourself in knots, when maybe you don't have to. Why don't you just get those blue-chippers in here for a visit—finesse it however you have to—and get them excited about you, your program, the campus, the area, movie stars, beaches, whatever. And *then* see where you are."

"Maybe."

They came. It wasn't really all that difficult for Pete—just a matter of finessing answers to certain questions as Jenny had suggested, leaving implications hanging in the air, being charming and subtly aggressive, dropping little hints or indications here and there. And here came Butch McRae from Chicago and Ricky Roe from French Lick. Just for a visit, to look around, meet some people, no strings.

They joined Neon Bodeaux and were immediately

taken under Pete's wing and squired around. They went around the campus, out to the beaches, inland to the mountains.

They went in around the movie areas and found themselves backstage while a TV show was in progress. And, their mind still humming from the sights, into their room came Arsenio Hall himself. He greeted them one by one, shaking hands. The blue-chippers were goggle-eyed.

"Yeah, by all means," Arsenio told them, rubbing his long fingers together and smiling his warm smile, "come on out to Western. You will have to *love* it out here. Understand me? If I'm lyin' I'm dyin'. We'll get you a pass to the show. You can drop by any time you want, hang a little. *Yes!* I want to see you here! We will warm . . . it . . . up!"

By the time they got to the Little Belgrade restaurant they were starved and exhausted and bedazzled. Pete had set them up ahead of time with steaks and the best service and various other little perks and touches.

"Another steak, Neon?" Pete asked. "Anybody? Hot fudge sundaes are the world's best, right here."

"Can I get more fries?" Butch asked.

"Are you kidding? Kay"—Pete signaled to the waitress—"fries here. One more New York strip, well done."

A bead of sweat ran down the back of Pete's neck, and he realized he was really revved up from a day's performance of whizzing these kids around and being the most interesting, supportive, exciting, inviting big-time college basketball coach in the country. He had his eye on a couple of men at a table in the far corner whose eyes, he had noticed, had been on him. He didn't recognize the faces, but he knew the demeanor.

He leaned over to Neon. "Those two palookas in the corner—don't look!—they are dicks with the NCSA. They got nothing better to do than to watch me like a hawk, hoping I break some little stupid rule they can bust me up for."

"Is this illegal, buying us dinner?"

"Not now. Not yet. You're just visitors. But after you enroll here as students, if you do, I can't buy you a doughnut."

"You can be generous when we aren't here and not when we *are?* I don't see the logic."

"There ain't no logic, Neon. One of the things you got to learn is that things don't run on logic. You count on greed, stupidity, and fear. That's what runs things."

The boys continued to wolf down dinner. Pete discreetly caught Kay's eye, and a few minutes later she came sashaying over.

Kay was an eye's delight in her tight pink miniskirt uniform, her long auburn hair swirling over her shoulders, her doe eyes painted dark and deep. "Well, Coach, how was the meal? Maybe it's time to tell me who you're with."

"Sweetheart, the meal was great. Butch, Neon and Ricky—this is Kay."

The three nodded hello. She was standing next to Ricky, and reached down to shake his hand.

"So, Ricky," she said, "you go to Western?"

"I'm thinking about it," he said, then cleared his throat.

"Well, that would be great if you were around here. Maybe I'd get to see a lot more of you. Nice to meet you boys."

Kay flashed her dazzling smile and turned to head toward the kitchen, swishing her hips.

"Wow," Ricky muttered.

Pete smiled sagely and leaned over to whisper to Ricky. "Southern California has an *amazing* supply. Blows your mind."

It was all too easy, Pete thought; Kay was all too easily satisfied with her twenty bucks.

After dinner he took the groggy athletes to the arena. It was lit up like a monument.

"There it is, gentlemen," Pete said, swinging his arm out grandly. "That's our palace."

"Whoa . . . Lookit. . . . Somethin'," mumbled the athletes.

"Students used to wait in line all night for tickets," Pete said. "We're on the verge of that again. You ever hear fifteen thousand people cheering for you? Come on."

He led them inside. The empty arena was lit up as if for a game. "Come out here," he said, striding to the middle of the court. "Come and stand right here and look around."

They gaped at the vast structure, the ocean of seats.

"See those banners over your heads? Those are our championships. Aren't they something?"

The boys looked up, awed, their mouths hanging open.

Pete stood at the scorer's table watching their reactions. He reached down and pressed a switch, activating a tape machine.

"Ladies and gentlemen!" boomed a voice from the huge scoreboard speakers. "The starting lineup for the Western University Dolphins!"

The boys looked around and at each other.

"At guard, six feet eight, from Chicago, Illinois, number twenty-two, Butch *McRae!*" A huge roar from an invisible crowd followed the announcement.

"At forward, from French Lick, Indiana, six feet eleven, number forty-three, Ricky *Roe!*" Another crowd roar.

"And at center, from New Orleans, Louisiana, seven feet two, number fifty, Neon *Booo-deaux!*" Again the roar.

The three players stood alone at center court in the empty arena, mesmerized and breathless.

Pete walked out to them. "Well, how was that? Nice, huh?"

"Whew," Butch said, shaking his head, "I like that, Coach. Only one thing wrong, though. I'm not that tall."

"I loved it too, but I ain't no six-eleven either," Ricky said.

"I know I ain't seven-two," Neon said. "But that's a

trip to hear your name like that. How'd you do that, with the crowd?"

"I am Mr. Magic, guys. And that's how tall you'll be when you play here. This place makes you feel ten feet tall. How'd you like to go a little three-on-three with the varsity?"

"Whoa! . . . All right! . . . Proper!"

13

THE VARSITY PLAYERS WORE THEIR BLUE-AND-GOLD
game uniforms, against the blue chippers in ath-
letic-department white. It was a ploy of Pete's to
allow the varsity players their pride and give the
blue-chippers added incentive to play against big-
time starters.

From the start, the blue-chippers dominated the
varsity trio of guard Tony Macklin, forward Michael,
and center Chuck. Tony was able to contain Butch
moderately well and to drive against him a couple of
times, but Michael could not handle Ricky, and
Chuck was hopeless against the size and strength and
quickness of Neon.

Assistant coach Mel, watching from the sideline,

was surprised; Pete and Freddie were less so. Pete refereed the half-court game, keeping up a steady chatter to encourage intensity on both sides.

Athletic director Vic Roker leaned against the doorway, curious about the action.

Butch made a fine drive against Tony, passing off over his head at the last instant to Neon, who thundered home a slam and brought his elbow down on Chuck's head.

Chuck stumbled away a little dazed, and Pete called for a break.

Mel waved Freddie over. "That's some good stuff I see out there, but isn't it against regulations to have high school kids scrimmage against the college varsity?"

"Technically," Freddie said. "But I figure, measured to the whole range of crimes against mankind, this is closer to jaywalking than murder."

"But still . . ."

"What, you gonna tell on us? Come on, this is nothing. Who're we hurting? Nobody. These kids are just having some fun. And I'll tell you what: it's a mismatch."

"Looks like the only one that belongs on the court with those guys is Tony."

"Yeah. Think if we could sign these guys up."

Mel shook his head. "I figured these guys could play," he said, "but I had no idea they were this ready."

"You know what I could do with these kids?" Pete

said. "Do you know? Man, oh, man. What a power-house. We wouldn't lose. And when you win like that, everything is better. Food tastes better. Your wife is prettier. Your—"

"Yeah, yeah," Mel said. "We know the speech. How close are you?"

"Oh, I think we're close. I think we could wrap up two of them, if not all three."

"Which one is doubtful?"

"I'm not gonna tell you. You're better off not knowing everything at this stage, right, Mel?"

"Yeah."

As they drifted off the court, Tony said, "These kids can flat play."

"You got that right," Michael said. "My career is history if these guys come.

"I'm on the line, too," Chuck said. "You *know* they'd love to get another white guy in here."

"He ain't no ordinary paleface," Tony said. "You can see Larry's been working with him—his shot looks just the same."

"It *would* be nice to win, though," Michael said.

At that they agreed.

"Rumors are all over campus," Mel said.

They sat in Pete's office, guzzling Perrier and cooling down.

"Such as?"

Mel chuckled. "We already signed five McDonald's

All-Americans, we already signed two, everybody turned us down—the whole gamut, as usual."

"It's no secret these guys are here. *Nobody* knows what they're gonna do."

"You got an inkling?"

"Oh, Mel, I don't know. I don't have the confidence in my hunches that I used to have. I think all three are possible."

"That's my feeling. What a coup."

There was a knock at the door. Pete nodded, and Mel reached up from his chair and opened it.

"Hi, Coach," Ricky Roe said. "Can I talk to you?"

"Sure. In private?"

"Naw." He came in and stood there a moment.

"Lot of great girls around here. You were right about that. I think I'd like to be on a college campus after all."

"That's good to hear."

"And I like this place. Pretty place. Nice."

"That's great. Well, then . . ."

"So there's probably a little business we should discuss."

"Business?" Pete leaned forward and rubbed his chin.

"Yeah, you know."

"I *don't* know."

Ricky glanced at Mel.

"Go ahead, son," Mel said, flipping his hand at Ricky. "Don't mind me. I don't know anything about business."

"Well, you know my old man wants a tractor."

"He made me aware of that," Pete said coolly.

"But I didn't tell you what I want."

"You? I was led to believe you wanted to go to college and play hoops."

"That's part of it."

"Okay. Give me the rest of it." Pete slowly rose from his chair.

"Look, I'm white, right?"

"Now that you mention it."

"I figure a white blue-chip athlete these days is worth something extra. Like Larry was."

"Like *Larry!* There *wasn't* anybody like Larry."

"Still, I do think that."

"Spit it out, kid."

"I want thirty thousand dollars, cash money in a bag."

Pete's mouth dropped open. Mel stood up and turned his back to them.

"You'd better be kidding," Pete said.

"No. I know you probably think I'm a hick, but I'm not naive about everything. I've been offered that much already, but I like it here better. I mean, I really would like to play for you. Honest. Just if you match that offer, I'm yours."

"Your father put you up to this?" Pete glared icily.

"Nope. He's just a farmer. He said basketball was up to me."

"You stupid jerk. You punk! Who do you think you

are? Who do you think *I* am? You never heard anybody say I did this! Get outta here!"

"But shouldn't we—"

"Get out before I staple you to the floor!"

Ricky backed out and could be heard trotting away down the hall.

"Whew!" Pete said, looking at Mel.

"Gonna be tough this year," Mel said grimly.

Pete walked. He steamed and swore inwardly and worked his fingers into fists. This was his favorite time of day, but he wanted no part of it. The whole stinking system was pathetic. What are we doing with our kids? he wondered. What are we turning into?

There were a lot of people in the streets, and he bulldozed his way right through them. He ignored friendly calls and waves. There were times when a man could feel lonelier than lonely.

What he wanted was justice. Well, what he wanted was success. Success ought to accompany justice. What we had was greed, stupidity, and . . .

Was there fear now, too? Was he afraid?

He walked through the door of Little Belgrade, went straight to the bar, and slid onto a stool. "Smitty," he said, lightly slapping the bar, "hit me."

"If I ask you what you want, you gonna make jokes?"

"No. Anchor Steam. First a shot of Bushmills. You know what, Smitty? It's stupid to drink when you're upset."

"Mmm." Smitty poured the shot of Irish whiskey and set out an open beer and a frosty mug. Then he leaned on his elbows. "I'm paid to listen."

"Not by me, barkeep."

"You don't want to talk?"

"Naw. I want to get loaded. A little, anyway. I'm not that upset. You have to think when you talk. I don't wanna think about anything."

Smitty chuckled and poured another shot and wandered off down the bar.

Pete drank for a while. And of course he did think. But it was not helpful. He couldn't think the way he wanted to think—that is, he couldn't come up with solutions. It didn't get better, it didn't get worse; he stayed grumpy.

Vic Roker strolled in and took the stool next to Pete. "Looks like you got a running start on me."

"Who's running, you fat turkey? I got nowhere to go. I've been trying to get buzzed up, but it's not working. Maybe I'm too old. Alcohol doesn't get absorbed by my innards anymore."

"That's probably it." Smitty put a draft beer in front of him. "So what's up, Coach?"

"I know how to deal with rules."

Vic waited. Pete was silent. "Yeah, so?"

"I can get rules to dance and twist and bend in the moonlight. I talk sweet in their ear, scream at 'em, threaten 'em, or crawl on my knees and beg forgiveness from the bastards." He threw down a shot. "I do everything but break 'em."

"Break rules?"

"Yeah."

"You don't want to break rules."

"Yeah."

"Pete, maybe I know where you're going with this, but I don't want to hear about it."

"What am I supposed to do, Vic?"

"I don't know. I don't want to know about it. Whatever you do."

"You're not going to help me out with some advice?"

"Nope, nope." Vic held his hands up.

"Not gonna talk me into one way or the other?"

"I don't want to know."

"Do you know about your football team?"

"I know nothing, Pete. Cut it out."

"You know what players got what?"

Vic turned away.

"Maybe if, well, just this one time, if I, you know. Maybe just this one time I could . . . things might get back on track."

"I know nothing," he said again, slapping a bill on the bar and walking away.

Pete raised a mock toast to the departing figure.

"You're startin' to talk like a chancellor, Vic."

A while later, Pete strode out the door.

He found himself in the arena. He wandered along the sideline of the court and took a seat in one of the folding chairs that together served as the bench. He scanned the beloved place, the banners, the stands, the huge suspended scoreboard. He was as empty as this building. He buried his face in his hands.

He heard sounds of cheering. He popped his face up and looked around. Nobody. Nothing. Then the sounds again and a band and thumps of a ball being dribbled down the court. It was all in his head.

"I'm going nuts!" he bellowed into the void. "Somebody lock me up!"

He hurried out of the arena and made a beeline for the house of nuts. Don't bury me yet, he thought. You wanna play, I'll play.

He rang the doorbell.

Happy Kuykendall opened the door. "Pete, what are you doing here? It's two o'clock in the morning."

"Oh, thank you. That's what I came for, to get the time."

"Take it easy."

"We need to talk."

"Okay, come on in."

Happy was wearing a white terry-cloth bathrobe, which for some reason ticked Pete off even more.

"I want to talk business," Pete said.

Happy smiled. "Smartest thing you've done in years. Sit down, sit down. Coffee? Beer? Drink?"

"Shut up and tell me how it works."

"You don't need to know the details. There are, shall we say, 'friends of the program,' who take care of everything."

"I hate the friends of the program."

"Relax. You hate losing more. Everything's gonna be fine, Petey. We're gonna be on top again. You're a winner, Petey. You should be winning. You *will* be winning again. Everything is better when you win."

"Put a cork in it. Just get it done."

14

THROUGH THE ROLLING FARMLANDS OF INDIANA RUM-
bled a flatbed semi. It barged through the morning fog
while the driver sipped coffee from an insulated travel
mug.

"Hey, uh, Ajax," came a voice from the CB radio,
"how's it look over your shoulder there?"

The driver slipped his mike off the visor. "It's all
clear behind me, far as I know. I've only been on here
for the last twenty miles, though. Who'm I talking
to?"

"This is the Pendleton Products that just passed
you, the red Peterbilt. I'm Dagger."

"Oh, yeah, I saw you. I'm Jingo. Take it easy, now.
Road's damp."

"Thanks, buddy. Get that tractor home, now."

The driver ground down through the gears and pulled into the driveway of the farm, his destination, and chugged up to the farmhouse.

Mr. Roe came walking off the porch, wiping his hands with a yellow rag.

The driver climbed down and checked the sheet on his clipboard. "You Mr. Roe?"

"Yes sir. You got my baby aboard?"

"You bet. My name's Jingo. Let me just bust open the chains and I'll back her down the ramps."

Minutes later the shiny green John Deere was on the ground. Four-wheel drive and four rear wheels and a spacious cab. Mr. Roe climbed into the cab, then reached around for the gears and hydraulics and special power supplies. He traced his fingers over the glistening gauges, the radio, the air-conditioning controls. The "hours" meter read all zeros. He stretched his arm, enjoying the space.

Then he opened the door and climbed down. "This'll do just fine, Jingo. Yes, sir."

Pete didn't sleep all night. He watched TV, flicking around ceaselessly through the channels. From time to time he dialed Jenny's number and got no answer.

By morning he was numb. He shuffled into the kitchen and filled the Mr. Coffee. He put two raisin-cinnamon slices into the toaster, got the butter out, and stood waiting. The coffee trickling down made him go take a leak. Then the toast was ready, then the coffee.

He took the coffee in a mug and toast on a paper

towel into the living room. He sat staring out the window at the reeds in his side yard while he polished off the meal. Then he slid a wastebasket out to the middle of the room and piled up the old newspapers by his recliner.

Then he sat mechanically wadding up page after page and pushing little one-handers toward the wastebasket. Soon he could figure a percentage—not bad, fifty percent went in. Practice, practice. The sun came up, outside became day, morning wore on. Pete wadded up newspaper pages and pumped shots into the wastebasket hour after hour. Soon he was shooting nearly sixty percent.

He didn't want the phone to ring. And when it did, he didn't want to answer it. And when he did, he wanted to hear the briefest possible message and then get off, so he could take a nap.

The phone rang at a little after eleven o'clock. He answered it, listened a moment, said, "Okay, okay," impatiently, then hung up and went into the bedroom and lay down on the bed and stared at the ceiling, waiting for the next call.

The huge, yellow Allover Movers semi rumbled down out of the mountains into the smog of the basin.

"Y'all comin' alive back there, sweetheart?" the driver called into the sleeper. "We're comin' up on ground zero."

"I can't wait to get back there myself," said the man in the seat beside the driver, yawning.

"Well, you'll sure wait until my wife ain't back there," said the driver. They both laughed.

"I think I wrenched my gut back in Chicago," the man said. "Still hurts."

"Long as it holds up for a couple hours here, we got a breather before we head to Sacramento."

"Let's get 'er done."

The truck growled through the streets of West Los Angeles and eased to a stop in front of a neat ranch house with a nice yard front and back, all fenced in white picket.

"Here it comes, Mama!" shrieked a girl at the front gate.

"Yes, indeed," Lavada McRae said, coming down the front steps.

The driver climbed down with his clipboard. "Well, Mrs. McRae, here we are, right on time."

"I could hardly sleep at the motel."

"Well, a couple hours from now, y'all'll have yer own household unloaded, set up, and ready to go."

A brand new black Lexus with a Cajun Motors sticker on it, followed by an older version, cruised slowly down Cane Lane past overgrown fields interspersed with a scattering of small houses that once sheltered field workers. The driver scanned the houses, looking for a number.

He stopped in front of a house where a huge young black man sat rocking on the porch. "Sir," he called, "I'm looking for number forty-three, but I don't see any numbers."

"This is forty through fifty," came the answer, "from when ten names were listed here."

"I'm looking for Neon Bodeaux."

"You found him," Neon said, continuing to rock.

The driver got out with his clipboard and walked up the steps to the porch. "You're Neon Bodeaux?"

"'Swhat I said."

The man reached into his jacket pocket and took out a set of gold car keys on a gold ring. "These are yours."

"What you mean, those are mine?"

"These keys are yours, that car is yours."

"Must be a misunderstanding. I didn't order no car."

"I just deliver them, sir. I get a job, a name, a description, and that's all. She's one sweet chariot. All the papers are in the glove compartment. Have yourself a pleasant day."

The man went down the steps, got into the second car, and rode away.

Neon stopped rocking and looked at the keys in his hand, then out at the parked Lexus. "Well, well," he said. "Imagine that. Somebody's bein' friendly."

Lavada McRae checked the paper in her hand and looked up at the Century City building. "This has got to be it, I guess." She went in and took the elevator to the eleventh floor. The smoked-glass door ahead of her bore the name Outlook, Inc. She went through the door and down a carpeted hallway to the fourth door on the right.

On the fourth door was printed Lavada McRae, Vice President, Community Relations.

She took a key out of her jacket pocket and fitted it into the lock, and, despite the name on the door and all the written directions, was surprised that the door opened. Carpeted. Track lighting overhead. Venetian blinds half raised to expose a view over Beverly Hills. On the desk straight ahead was the nameplate: Lavada McRae.

"My, my," she mumbled. "It's all come true."

The dual rear wheels of the John Deere raised no trail of dust, a good sign of damp soil nourishing the early growth. He drove around the perimeter of each field, luxuriating on his high seat inside the cool cab, testing the controls, acquainting himself with the gears and brakes and power lifts and floodlights. It was so quiet and smooth. He couldn't wait until plowing season to enjoy the power and traction of this fine machine. Tomorrow he would get Joe and Heff and Charlie over here to see it, so he could watch their tongues hang out. Right now he didn't even want to go back to the house, just wanted to ride.

A black Cadillac pulled into the driveway and edged to a stop at the house. "Don't waste time in chitchat," the driver said to the man beside him. "Drop it and leave. No questions."

"Someday," the man said, cradling the black briefcase, "it'd be nice to just take it myself and leave."

"Not recommended," the driver said coolly.

The man got out, went to the door of the house, and knocked.

Ricky opened the door.

The man handed him the briefcase, nodded, turned on his heel, and headed back to the Cadillac.

Ricky glanced out to the fields and saw the tractor in the distance. He hurried to his room and opened the briefcase. Amid the rustling filler of white plastic worms were six bundles of one-hundred-dollar bills.

"Yes!" Ricky yelled, raising a fist.

Pete sat in his recliner popping push shots of newspaper basketballs into the wastebasket. He had not shaved or dressed in thirty-six hours. On the coffee table beside him sat a pizza box with one slice left, and seven empty beer bottles. The light was dim, sunset over the Pacific.

Chunk . . . chunk went the wads into the basket. He was shooting almost eighty percent now. There were only a couple of old yellow newspapers left. What would he do if he ran out?

At last the phone rang. He picked it up slowly. "Yeah? Okay." He hung up.

"So that's it," he muttered. "That's all of it. Done. No big deal."

He got up, stretched, and went into the bathroom to shave and shower. He needed to take a walk.

15

ED AXELBY STUDIED THE FAX THAT HAD COME ON HIS personal machine. It was nothing conclusive, just a tip. But it jibed with his hunches and it made sense. Because the news that Butch McRae and Ricky Roe had signed letters of intent to attend Western University didn't make sense, especially when combined with word that that big lug Bodeaux who had been loping around campus on a visit also was coming here.

No, not all three. Not with the other offers he knew were out there for the two real blue-chippers, McRae and Roe. It was too sudden, too pat, too coincidental.

He walked over to another writer's desk. "Charlie, this smells, these letters of intent. Western got letters of intent from both Butch McRae *and* Ricky Roe."

"Plus that guy named Neon Bodeaux?"

"That's right. I don't have it all yet. Bits and pieces. But it's dirty."

"Naw, not Pete Bell. He's got a reputation over the years. Maybe he's got his old recruiting touch back."

"He bought 'em, Charlie. I know he bought 'em."

"You said you didn't have it all."

"But I'm sure. Give me a photographer. Let me have a couple of days. I promise I'll prove it."

"Hey, Axels, you were gonna prove point-shaving a couple of years ago, too. That turned out to be empty. You were gonna get Bell's wife to talk. Nothing."

"What's a couple of days?"

"No. No couple of days. Tell you what. You can play with this off and on. Around your other assignments. These kids are gonna be here all year. We'll take it a little at a time. I won't get in your way, so long as you pull your weight in here on your basics. Keep me posted."

In the Little Belgrade, Pete was trying to enjoy the toast Jenny was offering him when she raised her glass to touch his. This was their second glass of wine, and he had very much looked forward to finally having dinner with his ex-wife, even though his reasoning was fuzzy. He was not sure whether he was trying in general to win her back or not; he was not sure whether he agreed or disagreed with her characterization of their marriage. He was not sure whether she was good for him or he for her. But he had wanted to sit with her and drink wine and eat steak and talk about important things.

But he had not been able to relax and enjoy. He was edgy. He felt separated from her by a veil.

"You're back in business, coach," she said, clinking her glass against his.

"With me?" he said, his voice teasing.

"Don't get carried away. How'd you do it, Pete? What was the final key to getting the guys? Was it because they thought they'd be in the starting lineup here, given your record? Or just the old charm? Tradition? What?"

"There are some advantages to being fourteen-and-fifteen, I admit. We've got a good program. Lot of TV exposure. Nice campus. Nice weather. I don't know. Lots of reasons."

"Well, in any case you are to be congratulated for getting the players you wanted without becoming a pimp. You deserve the success."

"Yeah, well . . ." He studied his glass. "The rules don't make sense, you know. So many people are on the take. And I can't say I blame them, not really."

"No? You've never had trouble blaming them in the past."

"Well, it gets tougher, you know, all around. The competition, the pace, the dollars. After a while you can start to see that the process is inexorable. It's a marketplace."

"Not inexorable for you."

"Nobody's a saint."

She eyed him for a moment. "Why are you getting defensive about it?"

"I'm not getting defensive."

"Saying you're not defensive *is* defensive."

"But saying I *am* defensive means I *am* defensive. So if I say I'm not, then I am, and if I say I am, then I am. I'm in trouble either way."

"Pete, look me in the eye. You didn't cheat, did you?"

The abruptness of the question startled him. But he managed not to look startled. He calmly looked directly into her eyes and said, in a steady, sure voice, "No. I did not cheat. On a stack of Bibles."

"Well, then"—she smiled and raised her glass—"let's just not worry about it. We're a divorced couple out for a civilized dinner together. Nothing to lose."

"Right." He clinked her glass. "We got plenty to celebrate. I've got a real basketball team again. What a season it's going to be."

"And we're not screaming at each other. Not yet anyway, eh?"

"Waiter, more wine!"

Over dinner, and more drinks, Pete managed at last to relax. He got bubbly, in fact, giddy. He joked and teased aimlessly, now steering the conversation away from any and all topics of importance. He kept it as if they were two teenagers jousting on an early date. He kept things flitting around, not letting anything settle down for a good look.

She matched him in drinks and mood, and they left the restaurant arm in arm, giggling.

It seemed natural that they ended up at her house— natural except for the fact that he was aware of every tiny nuance of conversation and turn in the road that got them there. She turned on an easy-listening station, and they drifted out to the patio that overlooked the canyon, and he took her gently into his arms and they began to dance, or at least to sway rhythmically.

"Mmm, nice," she said into his shoulder.

"Just like old times."

"Just nice."

"Y'know . . . the world thinks I'm a mad man but I'm really so square Euclid could write a postulate about me—"

"Pete—" Jenny tried to interrupt him.

"And people think you're straight and old-fashioned but you're really much happier dancin' naked in the moonlight—"

"Would you shut up and kiss me?"

16

FALL ON THE CAMPUS OF WESTERN UNIVERSITY WAS NOT like fall on campuses in New England or North Carolina or Iowa. There were no changing colors, no chilly winds, no bite in the air. It was a palm-tree campus, a place of eternal spring. Students walked to class in shirtsleeves and sunbathed after class.

But it had the sports of fall and winter, and those sports were a very big deal on the huge campus of the Dolphins. Football was under way, basketball was in the wings; the athletes were in class.

Seventy-five freshmen, including a handful of athletes, sat in a lecture hall listening to a long-haired lecturer declaim on features of King Arthur's Round Table in an introductory course in classical literature.

". . . and as the razor-sharp blade of the sword of

Sir Gawain descends to inflict a mighty blow on the neck of the Green Knight," the lecturer emoted, "to the amazement of the steed of verdant hue . . ."

"What's he talking about?" Ricky whispered to Butch.

"Shut up and listen."

Ricky's eye roamed over the hall. "Oooh, boy, looka that . . . and that one over there . . . some true-life lovelies around this place."

"Shut up!" Butch got up and moved a few feet away.

". . . The head of the Green Knight, thus lopped off cleanly," the lecturer went on, striding back and forth on the dais and using his arms to demonstrate, "is kicked around the room like a soccer ball by Arthur's noble warriors."

Neon, his brow knitted, raised his hand.

The lecturer continued. "Whereupon the headless Green Knight strolls casually among Arthur's best and brightest, reaches down, picks up his own head, and places it back upon his shoulders, where it is magically part of his body once again."

He beamed a satisfied smile out over the students. Neon now raised both hands high in the air.

"This is a lecture," the lecturer announced resonantly, "not a discussion. So questions will not be entertained at this time. Please retract your hand. Hands. Now, then." He rubbed his own hands together and paced. "As the jaw of Gawain drops at the sight of the amazing capitation, the voice of the Green Knight suddenly fills the hall . . ."

Neon stood up. "I would like to speak," he boomed.

The lecturer stopped, his mouth drooping in a stagy frown. He raised a finger. "It is not your place to speak."

"I'm making it my place," Neon said.

"State your piece," the lecturer intoned, "if it's so important."

"I want to point out to the class that this course is culturally biased."

"Is that a fact?"

"It is a true fact."

"How is this course biased?"

"Why are we not hearing African folktales."

"Because this is a course in English literature."

"Why isn't this a course in African literature?"

"Why isn't it? Why isn't it?" The lecturer waved his arms awkwardly. "Because it isn't. It cannot be all things to all people. It is what it is and not anything else. It is"—he stiffened and shot a finger into the air—"because it is."

"Then I'll take it up with the curriculum committee."

"That is your privilege, sir. But we shall have no more debate in here. This is not a discussion seminar but a lecture. I speak, you listen." He looked at his watch. "We are out of time. Good day."

The students rose and milled around to leave. Several black students came over to slap palms with Neon.

"Crazy, eh?" Ricky said, shaking his head. "College is gonna be a strange trip."

"You got in his face, brother," Butch said to Neon. "You gonna get famous in a hurry in here, doin' that."

"I ain't trying to get famous in here. Let's get out."

Out the classroom door, down the corridor, out the building's front door. Smack into a television camera and a knot of people.

"'Sup?" Neon said to his mates. "'Sgoin' on?"

"TV's goin' on," Butch said. "We're goin' on."

"Here they come," said the TV reporter into his mike as the cameraman aimed over his shoulder, "Butch McRae, Ricky Roe, and Neon Bodeaux, the highly touted future of Western University basketball. The boys are fresh from their first class. Excuse me, boys." He took a couple of steps toward them, smiling broadly.

"Who you calling 'boys'?" Neon said.

"Well, uh, you *are,* um, I mean, could we have a word with you fellas?"

"I got nothing to say," Butch said. "I'm just trying to go to class. I'm outta here, Bo," he said to Neon. He ambled away.

"And you, Ricky," the TV man said, "how'd you enjoy your first lecture?"

"I liked the part where the guy's head gets chopped off."

"How's that?"

"Guess you had to be there."

"I have some things to say," Neon said. He took the mike from the reporter. "Mostly this place is culturally biased," he said, "and we have to work on that. You could see what I'm talking about especially in the Persian Gulf, where I spent some time. . . ."

In Pete's office, where he was going over some play diagrams with Mel, the phone rang. It was Tony.

"There's a TV station out there, Coach. They got the blue-chippers right when they came out of class. I—"

"I'll be right there!" Pete slammed down the phone and dashed out.

He ran across the campus to the classics building. He saw the swelling crowd at the entrance.

"Hey!" he bellowed. "Hey, TV! Hey!"

Neon interrupted his spiel when he saw Pete racing up, and quietly handed the mike back to the reporter.

"Hey, what do you think you're doing?" Pete panted at the TV man.

"Just doing an interview, Coach."

"Who told you you could talk to my boys?" He planted himself right in front of the cameraman, who lowered his camera.

"Nobody. It's just an interview. We don't need a permit to film here."

"You need *my* permit! You can't talk to my team without my permission! Don't you know that? That's an iron-clad rule. Who are you? This campus is private property! This ain't *Entertainment Tonight*. Get out of here!"

The reporter and cameraman backed off quickly, a technician scrambling to gather the cables they were stumbling over.

Behind them Pete saw Ed Axelby standing quietly, his arms folded over his chest. Behind Axelby was a photographer with two Nikons dangling around his neck.

"Hey, Ed, you cradle-robbing scum, you have anything to do with this? You behind this event here?"

"What's the matter, Coach?" Axelby said, advancing a couple of steps with his photographer, who was checking his camera.

"Don't give me that." Pete aimed a warning finger at Axelby. "Stay where you are!"

Axelby stopped and spread his arms innocently.

Several yards away off to the side, the TV cameraman had resumed filming.

"Axelby, you know you don't talk to my players, you canker sore."

"I'm not talking," Axelby said smoothly. "I'm just watching. What are you afraid of, Coach?"

A flash blanked Pete's eyes as the still photographer suddenly started snapping away. He lunged in that direction, blinking to see, rammed the cameraman, grabbed the Nikon, ripped it off the guy's neck, and slammed it to the turf.

"Bingo!" Pete barked. "Send the bill to the athletic department." He noticed the TV camera. "You get that? If you missed that action I'll do it again."

He turned away and stalked over to Neon and Ricky. "Look, you guys, all interviews come through me, got it?"

"Yes, sir," they said together.

"You think I was kidding when I told you that the other day, or what?"

They looked sheepishly at each other.

"I don't kid, boys, not about that. I become a serial killer. See you at practice."

"They need a lot of work, Mel," Pete said in his office. He had his feet up on his desk and was sipping iced tea through a straw.

"The chancellor's happy already," Mel said. "I saw Vic earlier, leading that little hair ball around on a leash. He says the chancellor would like you to stop by and say hello."

"Oh, no, not anymore. He wants to say hello, he can say it over here."

They both laughed.

"Okay." Pete swung his feet down and tossed the bottle in the wastebasket. "Let's go to work."

Pete drove them hard at practice.

"Swing, swing . . . pick up . . . Quicker, quicker! . . . Weak-side help, come on!"

His A-team so far was Tony and Butch at guard, Ricky and Michael Nover at forward, and Neon at center. Former starters Rafe Maskie and Chuck joined the others playing against them on the B-team.

Butch dribbled the ball over the center line to the top of the key, passed off to Ricky, and stood there watching Ricky work for a shot.

"Pass and move, Butch!" Pete commanded. "Away from the ball. Don't stand around, ever! And screen as you go. Motion! Motion!"

Butch set a screen and was easily shoved aside by Rafe.

"Tougher, Butch! Plant those feet! That's your spot! We don't have the Sisters of Mercy on our schedule this year. Move and watch the spacing."

The ball went in to Neon in the low post. He faked right, then left, then stood still.

"You waiting for Christmas, Bo? Do something with it! Shoot or pass, but don't take a nap!"

Ricky took a pass in the corner and went right up for a shot.

"Not everything's a shot, Ricky! Try a pass for once!"

Then he was back at Butch. "Stevie Wonder could set a better pick! How we gonna free up our shooters if you tiptoe around like this? What are you doing, Butch?"

"I'm not into your system," Butch muttered.

"Oh, really?" Pete walked over to him. "Well, I tell you what, Mr. High School All-Star, why don't we try *your* system? You got a system?" Butch looked at the floor. "Hey, Neon, how about you? You got a system we should try?"

"Nope."

"Then let's use Ricky's system. Naw, he doesn't have a system either, guys." Pete pursed his lips and shook his head slowly while he scratched it. "Looks like we're stuck with *my* system. My, oh, my. Guess we'll have to do what the *coach* wants to do. Think we could give it a try?"

Then he turned back to Butch and stuck his face up

close. "We'll try my system against people like Indiana, if that's all right with you. Okay? Good! We'll use my system and we'll work and work and work on it until it's comin' out of your navel, and if you don't learn it and run it the way I want it, you'll be running your own system down at the YMCA!"

He stomped toward the sideline. "Back to work!"

17

MEL, FREDDIE, AND JACK SAT AROUND PETE'S DESK in his office, hunched over to study some analyses of upcoming opponents, primarily those of their opening-night foe, Indiana, the team that the national press had been giving a preseason rating of number one in the country.

"Game's getting rougher," Jack said. "Refs are letting them bang more underneath."

"Everybody watches the Knicks," Pete said. "They're getting away with goon basketball, and the NBA is intimidated, thinks the crowds eat it up. The New York crowds, maybe. Not the rest of the world. I think it stinks."

"The kids copy that bully-ball, though," Mel said.

"It's easier to copy muscle than the skills of Michael or Sir Charles."

"Plus everybody's bigger and stronger every year," Freddie said. "The refs gotta control it."

"The *league's* gotta control it," Pete said, "both pros and college. I'm not worried about Indiana, though, in that regard. Bobby has 'em play disciplined and skilled every year. Nobody's gonna push us around anyway, with the heft we got."

"What you gotta worry about with Bobby Knight's teams," Mel said, "is just that they're so good. Every single time."

"He's as good a coach as there is," Pete said. "And he's got the record distance for chair throwing. I got the record for punting basketballs into the stands."

"They could smear us," Jack said.

"Yeah, they could," Pete said. "We got a lot to do."

There was a light knock on the door, and Jack got up to open it. "Hi, Butch."

"I'd like to talk to Coach."

"Come on in," Pete called, waving. "'Sup?"

"It's kind of private, if that's okay. Just for a couple minutes."

"Sure. Guys," he said to the assistants, "go down and grab some coffee, black for me, and then plug back in here." They left, and Pete motioned for Butch to sit down.

"I'm homesick," Butch said.

"That's normal. Nothing to be embarrassed about. Besides, your mother's here."

"It's not just that." Butch looked at the floor. "It's

bigger. I don't belong here. The West Coast. I don't know. I liked Chicago better."

"You don't like being yelled at, Butch. You gotta be tougher. I don't just mean setting picks and so on, I mean you gotta take criticism. The whole point is to make everybody play better basketball. That's all. You don't know how good you can be. *I* do. I know how much better you can be. That's why I yell."

Butch was silent for a moment. Then he looked up. "If I left school, would my mother lose her job and her house?"

"Is that supposed to be a serious question?"

"It's important to me."

"You're thinking of leaving because I'm tough with you?"

"You keep saying that. . . ."

"Listen, buster. I haven't even started being tough with you. I'm gonna ride you for four years—to a championship and a first-round draft pick for you, if you listen. Then you can live wherever you want to—Chicago or Sri Lanka for all I care."

"You didn't answer my question. Will my mother lose her house and job?"

Pete squinted at him. Without taking his eyes off Butch, he reached for the phone, put it in front of him, and dialed.

"Hello, it's Pete," he said into the mouthpiece. "I've got a question for you. Theoretically—just theoretically, now—if one of my guys, for whatever reason, decides to leave, what happens to the arrangement?"

Happy Kuykendall blew a gasket. "Arrangement? Arrangement, nothing! If some kid of yours is unhappy, it's your job to make him happy! Not arrangement, *job!* You wanna waffle, go find a waffle iron. Look, my friend, this is full steam ahead. No what-if's. You can sell ice to the Eskimos, and you can sell a kid on how happy he is. I know who you're talking about. I know everything. Butch's mother has a job and a house with a lawn, so Butch is happy here, got it? I don't wanna have another conversation like this."

Happy slammed the phone down in Pete's ear.

Pete hung up gently, his eyes still on Butch. "I think you better be at practice Monday. That's your answer."

Butch got up and silently left the room.

Pete stared after him. So this was what it was like, he thought, when the hooks were in.

Ed Axelby and fellow sportswriter Charlie Ireland leaned over a spread of photographs on the desk.

"Now, this here is Laverne coming out of their new house," Mark said, fingering a photograph.

"Lavada."

"Whatever—Mrs. McRae. And here she is going to her new job."

"Yup. The house is in her name with a cosigner who we can't locate. The bank officer who approved the loan is an alumnus of Western."

"Is that right?"

"Yup. Friends of the Program," Axelby said, "that's the group."

"Okay, and here's Ricky's father on his new tractor."

"We have no proof of anything except that Mr. Roe had bad credit—too bad to be purchasing expensive new machinery like this. And the largest distributor of farm machinery in the state of Indiana was a classmate of Happy Kuykendall, the alumni booster."

"He's everywhere, that guy," Charlie said. "Okay, here's Neon's car, the Lexus."

"The violations seem pretty flagrant but the paper trail on all this is pretty well covered." Ed leaned back and clasped his hands behind his head. "We know the football program isn't clean, but we never could prove anything. This is different. Keep digging. The paperwork is there. We're going to nail the great Pete Bell. That nutcase. That arrogant slime."

Practices got even tougher. When the players got tired, Pete lashed them in conditioning drills.

"Nobody is gonna be stronger than us in the fourth quarter!" he sang to them. "Nobody!"

When somebody bobbled the ball, he put them through loose-ball drills, rolling the ball in among them and having them fight for it, diving and scrambling on the floor.

"The prized jewel! It's worth your life! Nobody's gonna go after loose balls like we do!"

Players came up bruised and scratched. But fierce possession of the ball took on new meaning to them.

He made them run their passing offense without the ball touching the floor for an hour at a time.

He drilled them endlessly on picks and screens and weaves and switches, so they learned to move in flow like a single organism, each reacting instantly to the others, all attuned to the team.

On a defensive switching drill, there was some slow reaction. "You're dogging it, Butch. Quicker!"

Butch stared at him icily for a moment, but went right back to work.

Back and forth the ball went, inside, outside, around the perimeter, over the top. "Motion, motion! Eyes, defense, eyes!" Quickness was everything, everybody thinking all the time, no hesitation, flow, flow.

Neon took the pass in the low post, but instead of passing it back out, went into a complex, flashy move, faking left and right, spinning then to his left, twisting for the basket, sliding the ball in from behind his head. He slapped palms all around.

"What was that?" Pete yelled, running in. "No, no, no! We're running the offense, motion and passing, until I say otherwise!"

"You saying I can't go one-on-one?" Neon asked calmly.

"I'm saying first we learn the offense and the high percentage shots will be there too."

"You saying—"

"I said what I'm saying! You don't talk back to me. This isn't army ball. We're opening the season against

Indiana, not against the Belgian Nationals. The Hoosiers will be the toughest thing you've ever seen!"

"The Belgian Nationals?" Ricky mumbled. "Come on."

"Oh, now Mr. Roe has something to say?"

"Sorry."

"Sorry don't cut it, buster." Pete stomped back and forth, shifting the ball from hand to hand. "You and Neon run the lanes after practice. Fifty times." There was stone silence from the team.

"Now, as I was saying. I know every one of you thinks you're Michael Jordan and you have a lifetime to prove it to the world. But right now, for me, you ain't Michael Jordan and you ain't squat. And if you want to get beyond squat, you'll learn to move the ball and move without the ball. And on defense you're right in your man's face, and you talk, talk, talk to each other on defense. If you don't do these things, you won't even see the bottom side of squat. I don't want any cheap imitations of the great Mr. Jordan. This is not a shoe commercial. Passing game. Let's go!"

They drilled, became more fluid, more intense.

"No, no, Butch! On D you gotta either switch there or open up and let the man through—he can't go around behind you. Again!"

They ran switches neatly, clung to their men on D. Sometimes even too tightly. Ricky was guarded so close he didn't get open for a pass.

"Tony, show Ricky what to do when he's being overplayed like that. Ricky, play D on Tony."

Pete took the ball at the point. Tony went into the corner. Ricky was tight on him. Tony faked a move toward the ball, ducked behind Ricky, along the baseline, took a quick bounce pass from Pete, and laid it in.

"I thought you didn't want us to go one-on-one," Ricky whined.

"Aha! The lesson is, I want it to come out of the offense. Tony just moved without the ball. Got that?"

There were mutters of agreement.

"I am going to break this team of every bit of attitude problem it has. You will surrender your egos for the good of the team! So now I want *everybody* to run the lanes. Now!"

They ran from the baseline to the free-throw line and back; up to the midcourt and back; to the opposite free-throw line and back; all the way to the other end line and back.

"That's *one!*" Pete barked. "Again!"

Pete stood on the sidelines with his assistants while the boys ran forth and back, panting wildly, their sneakers squeaking a chorus as they wheeled and ran, wheeled and ran.

"When did kids start talking back?" Mel said.

"When teachers and parents stopped spanking their asses," Freddie quipped.

Mel chuckled.

"Indiana's gonna murder us," Freddie said.

"Yeah," Mel said, "all those seasoned, smart, mature, highly disciplined All-Americans. We don't have a prayer against Indiana, eh, Pete?"

"We'll beat Indiana," Pete said. "No question. Bobby Knight is mine."

Mel and Freddie gaped at him. Mel smiled and nodded.

18

THE DOLPHIN TANK WAS HOPPING A FEW MINUTES BE-
fore Pete's TV show. The Flagrant Fouls pep band was
beating out a march. Dolph the mascot was dancing
for the crowd that filled the seats. The light was on the
Hot Seat. The crowd buzzed with the news that the
three new blue-chippers—Neon, Butch, and Ricky—
were going to be Pete's guests.

Jenny entered through an offstage door and looked
around. Mel was watching preparations. "Mel?"
He turned around and smiled. She held out a
large envelope. "These are the Indiana game tapes
that Pete left at my house. He might not even know
he left them there. Would you give them to him for
me?"

"Sure, Jenny. Why don't you stay around for the

186

show, give him the tapes yourself? It's kind of fun watching offstage."

"Maybe I will."

Up near the stage, Pete was ready to go on. Jack came trotting up.

"We just got word," he said in a hoarse whisper, "Butch and Neon aren't coming!"

"Aren't coming? What do you mean? They're my guests for the show. They don't have a choice."

"I just got off the phone with Neon. Butch doesn't want to come, and Neon feels it's his duty to show solidarity."

"Solidarity! I can't believe this. What about solidarity with *me?* Are they nuts? What about Ricky? He can't even pronounce solidarity."

"I don't know."

The rear door opened, and Happy Kuykendall and Ricky sauntered in. Happy nodded and smiled at Jenny and Mel as they passed, and he continued beaming as they approached Pete.

"Mel," Jenny said, "What's Happy doing here?"

"You know, Mrs. Bell," Mel winked at Jenny knowingly. "He's just a 'Friend of the Program.'"

"Happy, a 'Friend of the Program'?" Jenny was dumbfounded.

"Well, you know how things are . . ." Mel said, realizing he'd gone too far.

"Give this to Coach Bell, please. And tell him I had to cancel our drink later," she said, handing Mel the envelope. Infuriated, she left him standing there without another word.

"We're here, we're here," Happy sang as Pete glowered at him. "Right on time. No panic. Everybody's happy."

"Not everybody," Pete growled, barely acknowledging them.

The show opened, and the blonde cheerleader cartwheeled out to the Hot Seat mike.

"Ladies and gentlemen, Dolphins, Dolphinettes, Dolphin fans, Dolphin nuts, and hoop lunatics everywhere. Your coach, my coach, our coach—Petey Bell!"

Pete strode onto the stage, waving as usual, slapping high fives with Dolph, and took the Hot Seat.

"Welcome to Masterpiece Theater, sports fans," Pete said, struggling to be lighthearted. "I know it had been announced that I was going to have the three new freshmen standouts here with me tonight. Two of them, however, Butch McRae and Neon Bodeaux, had scheduling conflicts. But we do have Ricky Roe, leading scorer in Indiana high school history, who broke all of the great Larry Bird's scoring records. And let's not wait around. Here he is now, Ricky Roe!"

Pete gestured grandly to the wings, and Ricky came shyly onto the stage, eyeing the cheerleader.

"How do you like things so far?" Pete asked.

"Hard work," Ricky said, too softly. Then, clearing his throat, he said more clearly, "Hard work."

"What do you think of the team at this stage?"

"Pretty good."

"Let's hear it for Ricky Roe," Pete said, steering him away toward the wings.

Pete kept the show short, answered a few dumb questions, roused the crowd against Indiana, and charged off. He charged straight at Happy Kuykendall.

"Great show, Pete!" Happy said, his arm around Ricky's shoulders.

"What are you doing here?" Pete hissed.

"Did I do something wrong?" Ricky asked, nervously.

"Not you—Hapless here. Let's move this." Conscious of eyes drawn toward the little scene, Pete shoved them down the hall toward a side room.

"Pete," Happy said over his shoulder as he was propelled along, "I think you and I should talk in private."

"I think I should leave," Ricky said.

"Okay, kid," Happy said. He slipped a set of keys into Ricky's hand and edged away.

"What's that?" Pete grabbed Ricky's hand.

"For a loaner, Coach," Ricky said, showing him the keys.

"You gave him a car? You gave him a *car?*"

"Easy, take it easy, Pete." Happy held up his hands and backed up. "Relax. A loaner, like the kid said. He's gonna give it back."

"Get outta here!" Pete barked at Ricky, who scatted off down the hall without looking back.

Pete shoved Happy backwards into the small room and banged the door shut behind him.

"I don't want you near my kids."

"Your kids?" Happy scoffed. "You sound like Jerry Lewis. Get your finger out of my face."

"I didn't authorize a car for Ricky?"

"You authorized the Friends of the Program to do what had to be done."

"Authorized schmauthorized! I didn't tell you to be stupid. Ricky's here, that business is over. You oughta be invisible."

"I'm being supportive."

"That farm kid's gonna flash that car all over town!" Pete stomped around the room. "How'm I gonna explain it?"

"You don't explain anything. You don't know anything. Tell the kid to keep his mouth shut. You're the coach. You just keep a rein on your end."

"I'd like to rein your end, you—"

"You'd better understand something, Mr. Righteous. I have few friends in this world, but the friends I do have are Friends of the Program and they are friends for life. What the Friends of the Program have done is untraceable and unprovable. My involvement is unprovable. They'll never find the smoking gun, because I am the smoking gun. The only mistake you can make is to go out of control on us and do something crazy and self-destructive—and destructive to these kids that we've helped, and destructive to the university that pays you so handsomely. That is to say, to put it simply, you should shut up and grow up."

"You're beneath scum."

"When you're finished with your juvenile name-calling, I should remind you that I have broken no laws. In fact, it is you who may have violated the collegiate Athletic laws. *Your* career is at stake, not mine."

"My career is in *my* hands."

"No it isn't Pete. I own you now. I can nod my head and rumors fly. About you, for example."

"Oh, yeah? Oh, yeah?" Pete continued stomping, clenching and unclenching his hands. "Rumors don't bother me. I've lived through accusations."

"Really?"

"Yeah, really. Remember the point-shaving crap two years ago? Nothing could be worse than that, and I came out fine and dandy, because I was clean and everything was clean. The most damaging allegation anybody ever heard of around here, and it was nothing, and I came out of it bigger than ever."

"Aaah, yes." Happy raised a finger and began pacing behind Pete. "The alleged incident. I have an interesting piece of news for you. It's true."

"What're you talking about?"

"Points were shaved."

"What?" Pete stopped and faced him.

"I bought one of your boys."

Pete slumped backwards into one of the armchairs, where he plopped down, open-mouthed.

"That game, January sixteenth three years ago."

"You're lying. No kid who ever played for me would fix a game! You're telling me something like that could happen and I wouldn't know about it?"

Happy smiled arrogantly, his chin high, his eyelids low, his nostrils flared. "Look at the game tapes. I own you, Bell."

Abruptly Happy turned and left the room.

Pete sat staring at the door, his mind reeling. It was just a lie, of course. If Happy was good at anything, it was at making your skin crawl. He rose and dusted himself off as if he'd just been in a fracas. He needed to take a walk. He needed to get to his office.

Pete's shelves held three-deep rows of videotapes. He went at them frantically, spilling the front rows onto the floor to get to the ones behind. At last he had January 16, 1989, marked with the opponent's name.

He put it in the VCR and watched the screen.

The game took on an entirely different tone from ever before. It had been a win—a little sloppy, but a win. So he had taken from it only the lesson that they needed to work harder on a few things. Now it took on the sinister quality of a Hitchcock thriller.

Somewhere in this tape was a killer. It would take an expert to see the clues. One of his players was the killer. Pete himself was the victim; his whole career, his livelihood, his life, was threatened by somebody playing basketball on this tape. Pete was the expert who would spot the clues. These players were like sons to him. He would be able to identify the killer.

If there was one. But Happy's mean words had struck him like the truth.

He watched the tape with an intensity that soaked his shirt. Slow motion of segments, back and forth over plays. He was not looking for mistakes. He was looking for intentional errors that would go unnoticed to ordinary eyes—even to his own when he was ignorant—but would jump out to him now. He was looking for a pattern of misplays.

Back and forth, back and forth, advancing slowly through the game. The pattern began to take shape. For a while he wasn't sure. Gradually he became sure.

Mel arrived, knocking once and then coming in and immediately fixing his eyes on the TV screen. "Sorry I wasn't home when you called, Coach. What is it?"

"Happy told me the shave was on. He bought a player three years ago, this game."

Mel exhaled slowly, eyes on the screen. "You see it?"

"I've isolated a few sections." He ran the digital counter back.

The tape showed Tony slipping through for a layup. He missed it. But the ball hadn't slipped out of his hand as it had appeared to do at the time. It was a controlled miss.

On defense Tony stumbled, his man broke free for a slam. It was a controlled stumble, manufactured.

On a fast break, Tony passed the ball far over Chuck's head. It was aimed where it went.

"I don't know," Mel said, biting his lip. "He was only a freshman."

"But the only blue-chip player on a very young team. The leader, even then."

"Tony's always stunk up the gym on defense—this was just another bad night for him."

"Yeah. Keep watching."

Tony lost his man, appeared to have something in his eye; Tony limped on a turned ankle, but a minute later showed no limp; Tony dribbled the ball off his foot and it went out of bounds, but his eyes were right on his foot as he did it. The pattern went on and became clearer and clearer.

"But we won the game, Pete. We won the game."

"But we didn't cover the spread, Mel. I checked it. The spread in Vegas was twelve points, and apparently there was heavy action. We should have won by twenty. We won by seven. Somebody got rich."

"Oh, boy."

Pete stopped the tape and slumped in his chair.

"But *who*, Pete? Not Tony?"

"No, Tony didn't get rich. I don't care who did. There's probably lots of rich who's. But Tony got paid. A little would have seemed a lot to him. And maybe to his mama."

"Oh, boy."

"Well . . ." Pete got up slowly, his face flushed. "I gotta go see Tony . . . alone."

19

THE SIGHT OF PETE BELL TEARING ACROSS CAMPUS WAS in wild contrast to the peaceful, relaxed surroundings. Students milled casually around lawns and buildings and porches, laughing, kissing, reading. Music—from classical to heavy metal—poured out of windows as accompaniment both to the casual mix of students and to the churning legs under the enraged and single-minded basketball coach.

Up Greek Row to the fraternity house in which dwelt a good number of jocks. Pete trotted up the steps, pushed through the group of students around the portico, barged through the big door, charged on into the corridor and up the stairs, and stormed through the door to Tony's room.

"Tony!" was all Pete could say right away, while he ground his teeth and his hands shook.

Tony sat gaping up from the edge of the bed where he sat with his stunned girlfriend, Evonda. "'Sup?" he said weakly.

"You . . . you—" he sputtered.

"Better leave, punkin," Tony said softly to the girl. She popped up and scooted out. "What's the matter, Coach?"

Pete shoved Tony backwards hard onto the bed and bent over him and grabbed him by the neck of his T-shirt. "You give me some straight answers, buster, the truth! You gotta tell me the truth!"

"Always, Coach."

"Three years ago against State did you shave points?"

"Coach, Coach, it's me, Tony, you're talking to." He looked up with soulful eyes. "Would I do something like that. Would I?"

"Shut your mouth! I asked you a question! Did you take money to shave points?"

Tony hesitated, meeting Pete's fierce eyes with gentle ones of his own. "No, I didn't. I swear."

Pete shook him. "You swear on your mother?"

"I told you, I swear."

Pete yanked him off the bed and hurled him against the wall, his head bouncing off a corkboard. Pete jammed his forearm against Tony's neck and pinned him there. "You did it! I can tell! I looked at the tape! I know you! You were my guy, and you did it! Tell me!"

"Just once," Tony gasped. "Once."

Pete eased his forearm back a bit.

"I'd never do it again, Coach. You gotta believe that!" Tony talked fast in a voice wet with tears. "They gave me eight grand. I'd never seen that much money. I sent it to my mother. It had something to do with gambling. But we won. I never would've let us lose. Not ever. Just keep the points down, that's all they said. But we won, I made sure—"

"Shut up!" Pete turned his back to Tony. "Haven't I always been there for you? Always! You had a problem, I was there for you, whether your girlfriend's in trouble or you're flunking TV or whatever, every single time! You're a better basketball player and a better man because of it. Is that right? Tell me! Say it!"

"Yes. But, Coach, please, if you tell people, I'll never get drafted into the NBA. Everything I tried to work so hard on will be down the tubes. Please don't tell. . . ."

Pete turned to face him. "And you lied to me! The game is what's left for you, and you lied to me! You lied to me anyway!"

He suddenly whirled and heaved himself against Tony's desk, lifting it, flipping it over, scattering books and paraphernalia all over. He burst out the door into a knot of students drawn by the commotion, shoved them aside, left the house, and raged into the soft L.A. night.

He walked and walked. Perhaps he gave the appearance of aloofness or vacant distractedness—stepping in the way of humming traffic, bumping into people—

but he withheld a storm that spun and raged and blew and rained and ravaged him inside. This wasn't even some backfire from his recent sin of allowing Happy Kuykendall to entice the latest trio to campus. This happened *before* anything Pete did wrong. Anything he knew of. Unless just being blind to the perversions two years ago cast him in the same guilt. But somehow, no matter what distinctions he might draw, it was now all bound up inextricably together into one evil package, him and Tony included, that could bring his whole world down. He couldn't even claim innocence anymore. He'd finally sold his soul, only to discover a world of sold souls, and getting out of this mess was going to take some doing.

He found himself at Jenny's door, and there was nothing to do but knock.

"Pete! What in blazes—"

"I gotta talk."

"It's one o'clock in the morning." She held the door only slightly open, just her face in it, instead of swinging it open invitingly, as she usually did, regardless of how much she tut-tutted about his visits.

"It's *me* here." He tapped his chest with his thumb.

"That's another reason."

"What do you mean? What's wrong?"

She glanced up and down the street. "You lie to the world, you cheat, you buy players, that's all your business. But you lied to me. You looked me in the eye and lied to me. Without a glitch or a hesitation. And I believed your lie. I still trusted you."

"I'm sorry. It's complicated."

"I don't even trust myself anymore, because I thought I knew you. But I don't. Don't talk complicated. You lied to me."

There was a silence. But she didn't close the door.

"Three years ago," Pete began softly, "Happy Kuykendall bought Tony. The 'alleged incident' was real. Tony was like a son, but he lied to me. He's just a kid. If Happy owns Tony, he owns me. I coached a game where the fix was in. That's three years ago. That's before I got involved."

"Not Tony."

"He admitted it to me. A while ago."

"No. Oh . . . I don't believe it."

"So you see? What I didn't do then is worse than what I've done now. Except for lying to you. What I did this season is not as bad as lying to you. Not to me it isn't."

"Oh, Pete, poor Pete. You've got a lot of things to sort out. I'm sorry for you, and I know you're feeling lonely and abandoned and probably scared. But I'm not your guy anymore. I can't help you with anything. And I need to get some sleep."

"Okay." He nodded for a while. Then he turned and ambled off.

"You're still strong," she said, not knowing if he heard.

Pete sat in the dimly lit empty arena, in his coach's folding chair along the sideline, cradling a basketball in his arms and staring up at the championship banners hanging from the rafters. He didn't know what time it was. He'd come here after trying to talk to Jenny, and he'd been sitting here for some time. Maybe it was three or four in the morning. It didn't matter. So long as it was night, the world was standing still, nothing was going on regarding his situation. Everybody was asleep. He could do anything he wanted.

He took a few steps out onto the court, held the ball out in front of him like a punter, strode once, and kicked. The ball soared up over the seats, finally landing high among them, bouncing around, whanging off left and right, ending up on an aisle stairway where it rolled and bounded back down onto the court.

"Good leg, Pete."

He snapped his head around to see Vic Roker, the A.D., sitting up in the stands behind the bench.

"Like the old days," Vic said. "Sixty, seventy rows, eh?"

"What're you doing here?"

"Good question. We've got to stop meeting like this. Back when I coached, the night before the first game each season I used to come in here just like this, late, when the world was asleep, and I'd think about the season opening up the next day, the surprises and disappointments that lay ahead. You know. Just thinking. Like you're doing, I imagine."

Pete let the silence lie there between them for a bit, unsure of himself. Then he said, "I'm in real deep, Vic."

"I know."

"You know?"

"Some of it. Enough of it. I haven't exactly been there for you."

"Aw, it's my mess. You did what you had to do."

"Well, that's a nice way to let everybody off the hook, but I don't know. I guess everybody has to feel their own way. That's another way of looking at it." He got up and came slowly down the stairs and sat on a folding chair near Pete.

They both stared at the floor. Every once in a while Pete bounced the basketball a single time.

"Maybe this all will pass with no big damage," Vic said.

"It'll pass," Pete said, "no matter what."

"Yeah. When I started coaching years ago, I broke a lot of rules."

"You did?"

"Oh, yeah. Looked the other way at the appropriate time, you know. Eventually the program got so strong I was able to be Mr. Clean the rest of the way, never even had to think about cheating. But I got skeletons, Pete. Yes, sir."

"In terms of skeletons, it's starting to look like Halloween around here." Pete bounced the ball, then looked over at Vic. "What do I do?"

"You'll know." Vic looked at the floor. "The moment the buzzer sounds at the end of the first game, win or lose, you'll know."

Pete stared at him.

"Now get some sleep, kid." Vic reached over and tapped him on the knee.

"I'll be along."

Vic nodded and walked out.

Pete stared off. There was nothing he could do now, between now and tomorrow's game, to solve any problems except those involved with playing Indiana. So his job was to focus: freeze out all other worries, considerations, challenges, fears, distractions. Think about the game. Only this one game tomorrow against the nation's number one team. When it came to this kind of concentration, this job of focusing on the game, nobody could do it better. Not even Bobby Knight.

No other night in the arena was quite like opening night. A sellout, of course, like most games. But more: the enthusiasm of the crowd was built on the hope that all things were possible. You could win 'em all; you could win the conference title; you could go to the Final Four; you could become national champions. This could be the start of something big. Every opening night offered these possibilities.

And beyond that, on this night, was the hope that this team, featuring three new ballyhooed blue chips, might restore greatness to the basketball legend at Western University. There had been too many years of sub-par basketball at a place where par was excellence.

Giant flags were paraded around the court— United States, California, Western—while the band played razzmatazz in the stands, Dolph the mascot roamed around bumping and grinding, and the cheerleaders formed a tall, quivering pyramid at center court. Elevated to the capstone position at the top was the blonde cheerleader, perched like a gorgeous crane, with one wondrous leg straight and one cocked up, arms flared like a lily, back arched, golden hair in eternal swirl, smile of 500-watt halogen.

The red sweaters and shirts of the imported Indiana fans served to isolate them behind the basket at one end like a sea of happy devils delighting in taunting the home-team underdogs.

The cheerful expectations within the arena could not have contrasted more starkly with the quiet nerves of those in the locker room deep in the underground vaults of the building. Silent as the cinder blocks that enclosed it, except for the breathing of the youthful warriors in their flimsy white shorts and singlets with gold trim, and black-and-white Man-o'-Wars, the locker room was a furnace waiting to be stoked.

Into the room strode Coach Bell and his assistants. Eyes turned toward Pete as he stood before his team.

"We got a job to do, boys. And we're not going out there to put up a good fight and claim a moral victory. There is no such thing. We're going out there to win. To beat the team that thinks it's the best basketball team in the country. There is enough talent in this room to beat Indiana. X's and O's and execution and heart and we can become the best team in the country."

He began to pace back and forth. Some eyes followed him; some stayed fastened on the floor. Pete focused first on one player, then on the next.

"Butch, the ball is yours. Bring it up-court in a

hurry. The first option to begin with is Neon. Pound it inside to Neon.

"Neon, you take it to the hole right away and hard. We pound it inside and take it to the hole time after time after time until they stop it. They'll double or triple down low because Neon's beating their brains out. When they adjust, Neon dishes back out to Ricky."

Ricky shifted uncomfortably on the bench and kept his head down.

"Ricky, the basket here is the same height as it is on your father's barn in Indiana. And it's the same height today as it was yesterday and last week. This is *your* hoop. You can light it up. A couple of misses will not stop you. Relax. Keep shooting. You can outshoot anybody in this building.

"And, Tony . . ."

Tony locked his eyes on Pete's.

"If they come out high on Ricky, we reverse it right away to Tony. And, Tony, you curl off and take that jumper you've been working on for three years. That's your shot. They don't know about that shot. It'll be there all night. We control our own destiny. We don't think patterns. We think situations. We execute!"

Pete paused for a time, letting the silence goad their adrenals.

"And the defense is all in our hearts, boys—just think about this. Indiana is over there wondering what we're gonna do. The country's wondering what we're gonna do."

His voice rose and he bellowed "I'll send a note

over and *tell* Bobby Knight what we're gonna do! I'll give 'em our offense and give 'em our defense 'cause it's not what you do, it's *how* you do it! We're gonna go nose to nose with them at both ends of the court and you're gonna play better than you ever dreamed of because I *demand* it of you!"

All of a sudden he turned and slammed his fist into the blackboard, a little harder than he meant to, and it shattered, and he thought he might have broken his hand.

"Let's go!" he yelled, and the players leaped to their feet and burst out of the locker room as if blown out of the furnace.

20

THE GAME WAS NIP AND TUCK, A TIGHT, GRINDING DIS-
play of excellent execution and strong talent and exact
coaching on both sides. In front of the Indiana bench,
Bobby Knight prowled the sideline like a hunched
bear in his red sweater; Pete strode along his own
sideline in his blue one.

The lead switched back and forth, but neither team
led by more than four. They were tied at halftime.
"I'm not satisfied with this," Pete told the Dolphins in
the locker room.

In the second half they pounded the ball in to Neon,
who dominated inside until Indiana adjusted, fronted
him more and more often so he couldn't receive the
ball. Ricky missed his first three jumpers from the
corner, then hit on six in a row. Butch ran the team as

well as Tony had at point guard, and when Indiana began to press Butch coming up-court, Tony took the ball and broke the press with slick dribbling. He scored off the curl, he passed off to Mike underneath.

And through it all, their defense hounded the Hoosiers. The Dolphins switched deftly, chattered among themselves to work unified, contested every shot Indiana tried. On the boards, Neon was awesome.

But Indiana had an answer for everything. They adjusted and readjusted. Their techniques were flawless, their passes sharp and accurate, their discipline as unshakable as ever.

With three minutes to go, the score was tied, 78–78.

Both defenses clung ever more fiercely. An Indiana forward went back-door, took the bounce pass, went up to jam the shot, and was fouled by Ricky. He made the free throw, Indiana up by three.

"We're okay, we're okay!" Pete hollered, clapping. "Butch!"

Butch angled over as he brought the ball up-court.

"Make sure we run the passing game if they're not in a zone."

"Got it."

Butch set the offense. Indiana was man-to-man. The ball swung fast around the perimeter to Mike, then over the top all the way across into the other corner to Ricky, who went up for a three-pointer.

The game was tied at 81 with a minute left.

Indiana missed a short jumper. Neon rebounded and fed to Butch.

"Slow it down, Butch, slow it down, use the clock!" Pete called.

Butch and Tony passed back and forth as the clock wound down, went under thirty seconds, under twenty-five.

Then Neon jumped out to set a pick. Butch cut off him and drove the lane and laid it in.

Western by two.

Indiana called its last time-out to set up their play.

Pete knelt amid his panting team. "We'll front them inside. No foul. No foul! Front them inside, make them take it from outside. Eighteen seconds, guys! Suck it up. On your toes for eighteen seconds!"

Indiana brought the ball up quickly, poised and patient. The point guard tried to penetrate, but Tony and Butch pinched him off. He looked inside; everybody was fronted. With seven seconds left, he drove again and then passed off to his wing, and the forward who had stepped back beyond the three-point line threw up an off-balance one-hander that bounced off the far side of the rim, then off the backboard, and dropped through.

The scoreboard read, Western 83; Indiana 84.

Pete motioned immediately for a time-out, and the team gathered around him with two seconds left.

In complete control, but shouting to be heard, Pete Bell rallied his players. "Awright, awright, awright, listen to me. We're gonna win, you hear me, we're not gonna *try* to pull it out, we're *gonna pull it out!* We *will* win this game.

"This is the play," he said, scrawling the *X*'s and *O*'s

on his chalkboard. "Butch, you take the ball out here. They're gonna be overplaying Ricky thinking we're looking for an outside shot. Ricky, here—away from the ball, pick this man. Neon, it's you, *you're* the man, off the pick. You look good in that uniform, Neon, you look great! You with me, Neon? Huh? You want it bad? Slam it home! We got it, we got it!"

The play worked perfectly. Tony cut off Mike's pick to take the inbounds pass from Butch, made two quick dribbles toward the top of the key, faked a pass to his left to Ricky, and lobbed it a foot higher than the basket and just to the right. Neon took the pass in full soar and slammed it through so hard the basket supports rumbled.

The game was over—an 85–84 win—and while the crowd went into tumult, the Western players leaped together and tumbled to the court in a writhing mass of celebration, hugging, slapping, waving fists.

Pete met Bobby Knight in front of the scorer's table. To make himself heard over the riotous, gleeful yowling, Knight bent forward to Pete's ear.

"Good to have you back," he said.

The players arrived in the locker room hooting and hollering, grins fixed on their sweaty faces, uniforms saggy with sweat. They were drunk with victory.

"Yeah, yeah, yeah!" Ricky yelped, slashing the air with his hand. "Chopped off their heads like the Green Knight!"

"Monster slam, Bo!" Butch yelled to Neon. "Monster!"

"I *am* a monster!" Neon crowed.

"We are a monster *team!*" Tony shouted.

"Shut the door, Mel," Pete said to his assistant. Mel closed the locker room door, and Pete held his arms up.

"Quiet boys, sit down."

They were quickly quiet, suddenly exhausted.

"Gentlemen," Pete began softly and hesitantly, "sometimes the rules make no sense. But I believe in rules. Some of us broke them together. I can't win like this."

The boys gaped at him as he slowly shook his head.

"No, I can't. Tomorrow I want to talk to each one of you individually about your future here and beyond." He nodded around at them. "I love you all very much. You played quite a game."

He turned and started for the door, but Tony blocked his path.

"I let you down, Tony," he said quietly. "It didn't have to be like this."

"I let you down, too, Coach."

"You won't let people down often in your life."

"Neither will you, Coach."

With that he walked out, leaving the players bewildered and blinking at one another.

Everybody was at the press conference, from Chancellor Millar down. Happy Kuykendall was there, with other beaming alumni. Phil lurked near the back. Most of the press were seated in the front. Many of the others stood. Vic Roker shook Pete's hand at the microphone.

Pete looked over the crowd and saw Jenny near the rear. He smiled a little at her, but everybody was smiling, so it wasn't noticed.

"Somebody must have a stupid question," Pete announced. "Come ahead."

"Sir?" a reporter in the front waggled his pen. "How did it feel to have Bobby Knight—"

"Enough!" Pete held his hands up. "I'm tired of giving idiotic answers to idiotic questions." He looked out over the startled crowd. "Well, here we are, eh? And a billion people in China have no idea. I'm a Dolphin. I love basketball. Sometimes the world doesn't make total sense to me. But basketball does, and that's enough."

While he spoke he searched for Ed Axelby. Now he saw him and locked eyes. "Go head, Axelby. Here's your chance. Let's have it."

Ed Axelby stood up. "Do you want to comment on the rumor that you arranged for an automobile to be purchased for Neon Bodeaux?"

There were gasps around the room.

"Not just an automobile, Axelby. A top-of-the-line Lexus, loaded." He tipped his head up and scanned the crowd. "It was fully loaded, wasn't it, Happy?"

Heads turned toward Happy Kuykendall, whose lips formed "You're finished" at Pete.

"And the funny thing is, Neon never even asked for anything. He just wanted to play basketball. He wasn't for sale but we bought him anyway. And the price was cheap, if you ask me. He got thirteen boards tonight.

Quite a deal. Maybe if we'd bought him a Ferrari, he'd have scored forty."

Happy's face was red and twisted, and he began flailing. His alumni cohorts wrestled his arms down and pulled him away through the crowd.

"Oh, yeah," Pete went on to the stunned, hushed crowd that had so recently been boisterous and ecstatic. "Cars, tractors, houses, bags of cash. I don't even know what we paid for these kids. They asked for things, and we gave it to them. You asked me to win, and I gave it to you. The chancellor wants to brag at the country club. Alumni are slaphappy, and the shoe companies are licking their chops because they're about to turn a bunch of decent young kids into corporate spokesmen. This isn't about education anymore, and it ain't even about winning anymore, and it ain't much about basketball. It's about money. And I bought into it, and I'm a big part of the problem."

He scanned the crowd. "How'm I doin', Chancellor?"

Chancellor Percy Millar ducked his head and charged for the exit.

"Well, we already said good night to Happy Kuykendall, and now there goes the chancellor! He's hurrying off to call his friends and brag about the grade point averages of our student athletes! Rats deserting a sinking ship."

The crowd was buzzing and nervous now, people looking at one another, newsmen scribbling furiously, cameras humming and clicking.

"I'll tell you something else—somewhere on some

playground in America right now a ten-year-old boy is dribbling through his legs, exploding above the rim and slamming it home with his left hand. And five minutes from now he'll be surrounded by agents and corporate sponsors and coaches and people like me drooling because the kid holds our future employment in his hands because that's the way we've made it! The greatest coaching job I've ever done wasn't tonight— it was last year when we were 14 and 15! Those kids played to the maximum of their ability—and that wasn't good enough."

This time he scanned the crowd for Jenny, but now he couldn't find her.

"I have become what I despise!" Pete roared. "And I'm here to say two words I didn't think could ever come out of my mouth: I quit!"

He stormed off the podium, knocking aside microphones and heads and hands. The sea of witnesses parted for him as if he were hot lava or a scary savior.

"I can't get out of here fast enough," he muttered to himself.

Soon he was out of the arena, hurrying through the parking lot, trying to distance himself from the departing throngs who were still irrelevantly cheering and celebrating. He didn't see Jenny, who, leaning against her car, watched him pass. He didn't see anybody.

He hurried into the soft night, distancing himself from the noxious revelry that had almost made him sick. He walked and walked.

He found himself in a vaguely familiar neighborhood, a run-down, depressing section that ironically buoyed his spirits. He enjoyed seeing no other white faces. He came to the Jefferson Street Playground, lit up and busy, and he leaned against the chain-link fence to watch them playing basketball.

He smiled as the typical symbolic and happy trash-talk reached his ears: "in your face . . . on your case . . . We got a mouse in the house . . . Grab air, Big Butt. . . . Grab *this*. . . ."

Eight players, one ball, a few guys watching, a few girlfriends. The almost forgotten simplicity boggled his mind. He was enraptured by the rhythms and talents in the basic game of basketball.

He didn't hear the car door close near him. He didn't notice Jenny standing beside him until she spoke.

"Great move, Coach. I saw everything."

"Yeah?" He studied her for a moment, then turned back to the game. "You were right. I am the lousiest cheater who ever lived."

"No coach should be put under that kind of pressure."

"You don't have to defend me. I knew what I was doing."

"Then why did you do it?"

"Because I couldn't remember what it felt like to win."

"So? How did it feel?"

"I felt nothing. This is the greatest squad I've ever had, and I felt nothing. The kids are gonna get hurt. It's all gonna crash."

"The kids'll survive."

"They didn't have a chance to be kids. Tomorrow I'll talk to them, hand in my resignation to the chancellor, and then . . . well, I don't know."

"You gonna be okay?"

He turned to her with steely eyes. "You have to ask?"

She smiled. "You're still strong."

"We'll see. Hey, you!" He suddenly was waving to one of the players, a tall, skinny kid with a square-top haircut.

The kid looked at Pete like he was crazy. "Yeah, you. C'mere. He's eating your lunch. Hot roast beef sandwich. With gravy. Y'know something, Jesus Christ never saw a basketball game but if he did he'd tell you to give Big Butt there a head fake and backdoor him—"

"Pete—" Jenny interrupted.

"I love this game," Pete said.

"I'll give you a call sometime," Jenny said, starting away.

"When the smoke clears, yeah."

He watched the skinny guy fake, go back-door for the pass, leap gracefully, and slam the ball through the hoop. The kid looked over and raised his fist.

Pete raised his, too.